"We can have it all back, Mia."

He slid his hand to cup my cheek. His touch felt warm at first, but quickly turned hotter. Suddenly, I felt him pulsing inside me, through my veins. This time it didn't hurt. It felt sensual and intimate, like he was rubbing up against my soul and embracing me.

I wanted to pull away but couldn't. I missed this too much—that connection and closeness. He was the love of my life, and as much as I wanted to tell myself that this was not the same man, the lie was what I craved. I needed to feel him close one more time. I needed to feel his breath on my neck and hear his soft, deep groans in my ears. I needed to feel his lips and cock and hands touching me everywhere. I needed to fill that hole in my heart and breathe again even if it only lasted a moment.

"This is what you want, isn't it?" Lust twinkled in his gray eyes. He pulled me in tighter, allowing me to feel his erection. "There, you see. I haven't forgotten you completely. And with time, I might remember everything. Don't you want that?"

PRAISE FOR MIMI JEAN'S *USA TODAY* BESTSELLING KING SERIES

"Complex doesn't even begin to describe the plot or the characters in Mack. I was pretty much blown away with the range of emotions portrayed as well as how swept up I became with the story."

—Sara, Harlequin Junkie

"The writing was so suspenseful and well done that I couldn't put it down."

—Leigh, Guilty Pleasures

"I am not doing this book justice here. Flawless read... Intriguing story line. Hot main male character...and strong female character."

—Smart Mouth Smut

"It blew me away."

—Books for Me

"Mysterious and Captivating."

—Book Addict Haven

THE FUGLY SERIES
(Standalone/Contemporary Romance)
fugly
it's a fugly life

IMMORTAL MATCHMAKERS, INC., SERIES
(Standalones/Paranormal/Humor)
The Immortal Matchmakers (Book 1)
Tommaso (Book 2)
God of Wine (Book 3)

THE KING SERIES
(Dark Fantasy)
King's (Book 1)
King for a Day (Book 2)
King of Me (Book 3)
Mack (Book 4)

THE MERMEN TRILOGY
(Dark Fantasy)
Mermen (Book 1)
MerMadmen (Book 2)
MerCiless (Book 3)

TEN CLUB

THE KING SERIES
BOOK FIVE

MIMI JEAN PAMFILOFF

A Mimi Boutique Novel

Cover Design by Earthly Charms (www.earthlycharms.com)
Development Editing by Latoya C. Smith (lcsliterary.com)
Line Editing and Proof Reading by Pauline Nolet (www.paulinenolet.com)
Formatting by bbebooksthailand.com

Like "Free" Pirated Books?
Then Ask Yourself This Question: WHO ARE THESE PEOPLE I'M HELPING?

What sort of person or organization would put up a website that uses stolen work (or encourages its users to share stolen work) in order to make money for themselves, either through website traffic or direct sales? **Haven't you ever wondered?**

Putting up thousands of pirated books onto a website or creating those anonymous ebook file sharing sites takes time and resources. Quite a lot, actually.

So who are these people? Do you think they're decent, ethical people with good intentions? Why do they set up camp anonymously in countries where they can't easily be touched? And the money they make from advertising every time you go to their website, or through selling stolen work, **what are they using it for? The answer is you don't know.** They could be terrorists, organized criminals, or just greedy bastards. But one thing we DO know is that **THEY ARE CRIMINALS** who don't care about you, your family, or me and mine. **And their intentions can't be good.**

And every time you illegally share or download a book, YOU ARE HELPING these people. Meanwhile, people like me, who work to support a family and children, are left wondering why anyone would condone this.

So please, please ask yourself who YOU are HELPING when you support ebook piracy and then ask yourself who you are HURTING.

And for those who legally purchased/borrowed/obtained my work from a reputable retailer (not sure, just ask me!) muchas thank yous! You rock.

TEN CLUB

PROLOGUE
MIA

I rolled out of bed, feeling unrested and sore and out of my mind with grief. It had been another rough night for me, one of many to come, I assumed. But what else could I do?

You'll find coffee. Then you'll try to find a way to keep breathing. Because that was what widows did.

As I stumbled toward my bedroom doorway to go check on the baby, the phone rang on my nightstand. The caller ID said *Mack.*

"Hello?"

"Mia, I don't know how to say this, but he didn't stay dead. He's back, but he's not him anymore."

"What?" I blinked. "Could you repeat that?"

"King is back, Mia. And he made it clear he's not letting me end 10 Club."

"I'll call you," I started hyperventilating, "back," and passed out.

CHAPTER ONE
KING

Tonight calls for a celebration. No, it is not a birthday nor an anniversary. Men like me do not give a dark fuck about life's shitty little milestones. We care only for power or money—same fucking thing. And after tonight, I will have enough of both to break the fucking world.

"Hey, baby," says the topless bleach blonde rubbing her ass on my cock over my black slacks to the beat of the music, "I'm free after work."

"Shut up and keep dancing." Women like her don't come close to doing it for me, but she is the hottest, most expensive stripper in this private bar. A thousand dollars a minute. It's pocket change to me; however, everyone here tonight now wonders why I'm treating myself.

Just as I hoped.

My eyes sweep the smoky, dimly lit bar filled with 10 Club members sitting at little tables, whispering in the shadows, making their deals and bartering for whatever sadistic crap will get them off tonight—sex slaves, drugs, torture, murder, whatever. Anything goes. Of course, they're all talking about me, as well.

I smile and take a long victory drag off my cigar, ceremoniously blowing the smoke into the air above. I want them all to see me gloating. I want them talking to the other degenerate 10 Club fucks and speculating what I am up to. Because regardless of what it is, they'll all want to steal it from me. They'll all want a piece.

I'm counting on it.

"That's enough." I push the blonde's ass forward, rise from my seat, and straighten my blood red tie. I've done what I came for and can already hear the phones vibrating with speculation around the world at the hundred other 10 Club establishments like this one. "*King is here.*" "*Something's going down.*" "*What do you know and what's the price?*" they're all saying.

They'll never guess. Not in a million years.

I toss a thick roll of hundreds at the stripper, who goes on her hands and knees to fetch it from the floor. I can feel her lust-filled eyes on me as I step over her like the dog she is. After all, she's 10 Club property, not even human in my eyes. But she made her choice. We all have. No one is part of this debauchery by accident. That's not to say some aren't backed into impossible corners, forced to choose between things such as death or becoming part of our secret society comprised of two levels—

the powerful and the powerless.

Make that three levels. Because there's me. At the top.

I stroll toward the set of heavy iron doors and make my exit into the dark alley. It's raining and windy. Typical for a January in San Francisco. Personally, I like the somber feel of this weather— fits my mood. *Dark as fuck.*

I am ten steps from my sleek black Mercedes when I hear footsteps splashing through puddles behind me. From the sound of the short strides, I know it's a woman.

Fucking idiot. Doesn't she know I despise desperation? And I definitely don't pay to fuck strippers who are owned by 10 Club. *God only knows where that pussy's been.*

I shake my head, pulling my keys from my pocket, and hit the unlock button on the remote. "Sorry, sweetheart. Not interested."

"You're King, right?"

The soft voice is unfamiliar, so I turn my head. She's petite, blonde, and mildly interesting to look at; however, it's hard to tell just how interesting since she's wearing a garish yellow raincoat.

"Who's asking?" I say.

"Yes or no," she replies with a hint of a growl in her sweet voice.

My, my. Aren't we a demanding little thing? I decide to play along. Of course, she has no clue I can snap her neck with the twitch of my fingers.

"Let us pretend for a moment that I have replied with a yes. What's in it for me?" I ask.

She steps closer, which definitely draws my attention. Most people fear me. They don't know why, they often don't even realize it, but they definitely fear me. This one doesn't seem afraid.

Either that or she's too desperate to notice she's in the presence of something black hearted.

"They say you are the man who can find anything or anyone for a price," she says.

I like the way this conversation is moving. It means she wants something, and now that the streetlamp above has given me a better look at her luscious little lips, I'm fairly sure we can come to some sort of arrangement.

I cock a brow, silently urging her to continue.

"I-I need help finding someone."

Someone very important, I hope. Because I think I might like to add you to my collection. I collect many things, including people, although usually not for sex. I can get that without having to take on the responsibility of ownership. *But for her, I might make an exception.* Her wavy, shoulder-length blonde hair and wide blue eyes are at the top of my list when it comes to turn-ons, but what really gets me off are naivety and fearlessness. *She has plenty of both.*

"Go on," I say.

"I want you to help me find my husband."

Tonight just got a whole hell *of a lot more interest-*

ing. Because I love taking things that don't belong to me, and I sure as hell love breaking a person's soul.

I dip my head to give her a good look. She should see the face of the man who will be fucking her for the next few years until I grow tired of her and trade her away to another club member, likely one of those sick fuckers who enjoys making lampshades from women's legs and breasts. Like I said, anything goes in 10 Club, just as long as you've got ten billion in the bank and money to pay your dues—one billion a year—which buys you complete immunity from any government anywhere in the world. Of course, we own all the governments. How do you think so many sadistic pricks make it into office? Power and money are everything.

I lean down and let her drink in my dark features. *Yes, look into my eyes, sweetheart. See the promise of suffering in their cold gray depths.* But as I stare back at her, there's nothing. No fear in her eyes. No sadness or desperation. She's void of all emotion.

Tonight just got a whole hell *of a lot less interesting.* It's no fun for me if they're already broken.

"Sorry. I'm busy." I turn away and pop open the driver-side door.

"Wait. Aren't you going to help me?"

"I could," I say blandly, sliding into the cool leather of the driver's seat, "however, as you've pointed out, I am the man who can find anyone or anything for *a price*. You don't have anything I want."

She wedges herself between me and the car door I'm about to close. "Name it. Name your price, King." She grabs my shoulder and my groin floods with heated lust. Is it because she's not the least bit afraid and should be? Probably. Like I said, fearlessness and naivety make my dick hard.

I look up at her, deciding to make an offer though I would probably be better off going home to enjoy a bottle of expensive scotch and prepare for my dinner party. No. I won't be cooking or cleaning. I have slaves for such mundane bullcrap. This preparation is something else entirely.

"My price is you," I say, thinking she might make an interesting toy.

She doesn't bat an eyelash, which is surprising. They usually look a little offended or shocked when I tell them I'd like to own them.

"No deal," she says.

I shrug and start the engine. "Then I'm afraid we must part ways. Good luck finding him."

"I have money. A lot of money."

"Not interested." I'm already obscenely wealthy and will soon have the kinds of funds that make or break GDPs of first world countries. Whatever cash she's got is a pittance.

I give her a push and send her stumbling back so I can close the door.

"Wait!" She gets her footing straightened out and comes at me again. I almost admire her persistence. Almost.

"I have a ring," she announces. "I'm told it can keep a person from dying."

I push back on the heavy door to prevent it from slamming into her. She's got my attention. A man like me is always interested in items that bring back the dead or prevent people from dying once I do. *Especially now.*

I turn off the engine, slowly step from the car, and look down at her as she shrinks back a few feet. That's when I notice something's different about her. The light doesn't quite touch her, but instead reflects off a nearly undetectable sheen of energy surrounding her.

And we're back to a very interesting evening, indeed. People like her are rare. In fact, they are nearly extinct. I might have had something to do with that, but what can I say? In my younger years, I wasn't a fan of her people.

"How did you come about such an object?" I ask.

She lifts her delicate chin defiantly. I fucking love it. She's dancing with the devil and showing such bravery.

"None of your business."

Such bravado. I chuckle. "All right then, how do you know it works?"

"I just know. Do we have a deal? Yes or no,

King."

That sounds like something I might say, so I appreciate it. "I confess I am intrigued; therefore I will say yes. However, I should warn you that welshers are shown no mercy. If you do not deliver, for any reason, you will belong to me, and I won't be kind."

The woman freezes.

Ah, there it is. Fear. My black heart tingles with delight. *Now we are getting somewhere.*

"I won't back out," she says. "And the ring will work."

"Very good." I slide a card from the inside pocket of my coat and hand it over. "Be here tomorrow night at eight. I'm throwing a dinner party."

"I-I don't understand."

"I'm a busy man. You want me to find your missing husband, then we work when and where I say. That's the deal. Take it or leave it." Of course, that's a complete lie. I have no intention of helping her, but she will most certainly be useful to me. In fact, she's exactly what I've been needing. *Saves me the trouble of having to kill my brother's woman. For now.*

She nods in compliance.

"Very good. And don't be late. Ever." I return to my car, close the door, and restart the engine, realizing that she's simply standing there staring at me and that I've forgotten something.

I lower the window. "What's your name?"

She suddenly looks like someone has punched her in the stomach—a pained stillness in her face, and shoulders hunched forward like she wants to be sick. I'm guessing it's all sinking in. *Yes, sweetheart, you've just made a deal with the devil.* Actually, I'm worse. A thousand times over. There is no divine creation in my past. No possibility of regaining my wings. I am the sort of man who makes this world a horrible place to live in.

Not even death dares to fuck with me.

I look at the little woman, wondering what the hell she's waiting for. "Well?"

"Mia. My name is Mia Turner."

CHAPTER TWO
MIA

This can't be happening. I walked away from King, heading down the dark alley, feeling his soulless eyes burning through me until I turned the corner. Those eyes, once a stunning blue filled with vitality, were now a cold pale gray. His heart, once loyal and protective, had turned cruel and greedy. Everything else looked the same, however. Tall, lean muscled frame draped in a power suit. Jet black hair and dark thick lashes. An elegant, handsome man that screamed old-world money.

A monster in sheep's clothing.

Once out of sight, I doubled over, trying not to throw up. Whatever had happened to King made him darker, more sinister than ever, and it broke my fucking heart.

My breathing barely under control, I forced myself upright and slid my phone from my coat pocket to call the only person in the world I trusted: Mack.

It rang less than a second before I heard that deep familiar voice.

"I found him, and you were right." My voice came out shaky. "It's not him anymore. Or it is him, but something's happened. What's going on, Mack? Please tell me you know."

"Breathe, Mia. I can't understand you. And why the *fuck* did you go and see him? I told you he's dangerous."

Being King's twin brother, Mack would know. Less than a week ago, King had paid Mack and his fiancée a visit. The message was simple: "Stay the fuck out of my way, or I will kill you."

Mack wanted to dismantle 10 Club—the most vile, twisted group of people on the planet. Apparently, King didn't like that idea. Not entirely shocking for many complicated reasons, except for one small fact: King died. I'd been mourning him for days, trying to make sense of the pain.

And now he's back.

I was here in San Francisco because I had to see it with my own eyes. How had he done it? To the touch he felt warm and solid. It even smelled like him, but I could tell he wasn't really alive. Not in the traditional sense of the word, anyway.

"What happened, Mack? And why does King remember you but not me?"

"I don't have a damned clue, Mia."

"So what are we going to do?" I asked.

"I know you love my brother, but—"

"No, don't say it. Don't you dare talk about love, Mack. Not after what he did to me." I squeezed my lids tight, but the tears came out anyway, mixing with the raindrops on my cheeks.

No. Don't cry. You're done with all that, I told myself.

I ran the back of my hand under my eyes, trying to see straight, think straight, breathe straight. King had been the love of my life. Or so I'd thought until he traded my happiness and heart to save Mack.

Yes. He chose his brother's life over his own and over being with me.

No, I wasn't being petty. No one could ever accuse me of that after everything I'd been through for King.

Having lost my own brother over a year ago, part of me understood King's choice. The other part never would because the fact remained that this wasn't the first time King had died. Nope. He'd died long ago, trying to save his people. He'd then spent the next three thousand as a cursed, dark, disembodied soul trying to come back. All the while, he learned how to fool the living into think-ing he was alive. The man had powers that defied every rule of the universe.

And when the opportunity presented itself to me—to bring back a life—I had to choose. My brother or King.

I chose King.

I gave him that life! Me. I traded a piece of my soul for it, goddammit. For as long as I lived, my parents and I would mourn my brother, Justin. And for what?

After I heard that King had traded his life away and that the nature of his death would prevent him from ever returning, I'd been beyond consoling. I couldn't believe that someone so strong would ever die or that he would leave me without answers. Then his mark faded—a *K* he'd tattooed on my wrist that connected us physically and mentally.

He was gone. Really gone. And I was broken.

Mack lowered his voice. "I understand what you went through when he died, but whoever he is now, he's beyond our reach, Mia. And this is bigger than you, him, or me. He has to go. Otherwise my plan to dismantle 10 Club falls apart. I'm sorry, but there's no other choice."

I cleared my throat. "I think you misunderstood. You can send that fucker back to hell or wherever he came from, but not until I get what I want."

A prolonged silence marked Mack's surprise. "What do you want?"

"I want him to remember me so when I help you end him, he knows he was betrayed by the brother he sacrificed everything for and by the woman he lied to."

"You can't make this about revenge," he said. "You and I and anyone connected to us will never be safe as long as 10 Club is around."

I wasn't afraid of them, but Mack's perspective came from a different place. He'd been one of those slaves. He still had nightmares of the things his "owner" did to him.

"Mack," I said firmly, "I agree. They need to go away. But what about me? What about my justice?"

He grumbled a curse. "I won't allow you to risk your life because you're hurt or angry and not thinking straight. King has to die as quickly as possible."

Hurt and angry? No. I was fucking livid. I was dementedly pissed off. And yes, I was definitely not thinking straight. I was out of my goddamned fuming mind.

I ran my hand over my rain-drenched hair, shivering with a gust of icy, wet wind. I needed to get to my car—an airport rental—but with my head filled with so much chaos, I couldn't quite remember where the hell I'd left it or what the damned car looked like. Everything from the point where I'd received the phone call at home, about King being back, to the point when I saw him just now, all felt like a bad acid trip. Not that I would know, but I imagined.

My bad trip is still going... "Okay. And then what? What happens when you kill King?" I asked.

"I pretend to be him, take his place, and kill off the members. All I need are names, which King might have hidden somewhere since he manages the club's money."

I wondered how Mack could be so strategic yet casual about killing his brother. The two were connected in ways I couldn't begin to understand. My best guess was that Mack didn't truly believe it would ever be over for King. He'd come back twice now. Perhaps he'd come back again after Mack had taken care of 10 Club.

"All I'm asking is to give me a week. Just one week," I said.

"To do what?"

"I want to make him remember. I want to know why…" I couldn't finish my sentence without feeling like a broken, pathetic woman scorned even if my emotions were justified.

"For fuck's sake, Mia," he growled, "he will kill you if you so much as bat an eyelash the wrong way or displease him. That man is *not* King. He is *not* my brother. He is the fucking devil."

"You don't know what he is, and you have no right to tell me what to do."

Mack drew a steady breath and let it out with a loud groan. "Is there anything I can say to keep you away from him?"

"No."

"Then I'll give you a week, but there's one condition."

"What?"

"I need you to get into his warehouse and find lot ninety-four."

Oh, God. Not the warehouse. Bad, bad things lived inside that three-story building, and they would eat you alive if you were not welcome.

"What's lot ninety-four?" I asked.

"I don't exactly know."

A hard, ice-cold shiver rippled through the deepest layers of my skin. He was lying. I could feel it. Why would Mack lie? I trusted Mack, and now he didn't trust me?

I swallowed back my anger, realizing I was all on my own.

He continued, "It's something King mentioned once in passing. I'm hoping I can use it to put an end to 10 Club."

More lies. I could hear it in his voice.

"Sure. I'll do what I can," I lied, thinking I might try to get the mystery object du jour but would refrain from handing it over. If Mack wasn't coming clean with me, it was for a reason—our interests conflicted. And it didn't matter if Mack loved me. He was stubborn, just like his brother, and he always did what he thought was best. "I might need more than a week, though. King doesn't know me, so he's not just going to give me the keys."

"One week, Mia."

"It might not be possible."

"You seduced him once. Do it again."

Seduce King? I pinched the bridge of my nose. This version was far more evil and cruel than the man I once knew who had been cursed, dead, and searching for salvation. Even then, when he'd lived in pain for so long, there had been good inside him, fighting to stay alive. That was the piece of him I fell in love with, and it was gone now. I couldn't fathom trying to fake my lust, and even if I could, he'd see right through me. The best I could manage would be to mask my rage and keep my true feelings hidden.

"I'll figure it out some other way," I said.

"You always do. Call me in a few days with an update. And be careful, Mia. I can't be there to save you."

The call ended, and I refrained from tearing out my hair or yelling at the top of my lungs. Instead, I laughed with bitterness and looked up at the dark sky, letting the rain rinse the salty tears from my freezing face.

How could I pull this off? Because hell would freeze over before I allowed King to touch me again. I'd rather die than look into those hypnotic gray eyes that were once a sparkling blue when he was alive. I would do everything in my power to keep my sentimental emotions—the searing lust I once had, the profound love and trust we'd shared— under lock and key. I would have to play this another way: Beat him at his own game.

And this time, I knew his tricks. After all, I was his wife.

CHAPTER THREE

I had been to this home only once prior to King having it remodeled. Not because King hadn't invited me, but because he'd owned it for over two hundred years and to say the house had an unsettling vibe was a giant sugarcoated understatement.

Why?

It's difficult to explain, but before I met King, I was a twenty-five-year-old marketing manager who never quite fit in. Don't get me wrong, I did well and my peers liked me, but my empathy for others and caring nature were not considered valuable traits in such a cutthroat environment, so I always suppressed them. But when I met King, he opened my eyes and helped me understand that I was a Seer, the product of a long bloodline of women who possessed various abilities. Me, I could see things that the naked eye couldn't. So King saw me as his personal bloodhound. I would find items he wanted. He would help me find my missing brother, now deceased. Oh, and King would own me.

Desperate times. And the beginning of a very long, complicated relationship, one where I eventually had to give up my gifts—another long, complicated story that involved staying alive. In the end, however, I ended up with King. A man who walked into a room and made you feel equal parts lust and fear. Three-thousand-year-old kings could do that to a person.

Anyway, the first time King brought me to his elegant San Francisco home, sitting high on a hill overlooking the Golden Gate, my skin iced over and my heart turned galloping mad. My entire body violently protested being anywhere near the place, and I'd refused to ever go back.

Until now. Yippy.

I approached the clear glass front door, taking careful steps up the cement walkway in my three-inch red heels and long red satin dress with matching evening bag. King once bought a similar outfit for me, and I hoped it might jar his memory though I had no clue why he'd lost it.

I rang the doorbell and stepped back, craning my neck to gaze up the towering façade of the freshly remodeled home, now a modernist affair of smooth white stucco, stainless steel, and glass. King had trashed his old Victorian for some strange reason, but the vibe remained unchanged.

Creepy as fuck.

A twiggy woman wearing a skin-tight black pantsuit, her dark hair slicked back into a sleek bun, sashayed to the door. She had elegant bones, deep olive skin, and vacant eyes. Her disposition reminded me of a 10 Club slave, but her physical characteristics reminded me of King's servants back in Crete, his home where I now lived. No, he hadn't returned since his most recent death, and I doubted he would. For some reason, anything having to do with me no longer existed in his mind.

Why? I could only make wild guesses.

The woman flashed a flimsy smile with her bright red lips and slowly looked me over. I'd worn my long blonde bob curly, just the way King liked, and I'd put a little bronzer on my pale cheeks. I guess I didn't look fancy enough by her standards.

Too bad. I wore a dress and that was about as fancy as I got.

"Ms. Turner," she said with snit, "King is displeased you are late. He says I am to pour you a stiff drink and you are to join him immediately."

I'd come late on purpose. There was once a time I wouldn't dare defy this man, but those days were over.

This time, we're playing by my rules. He was going to hate that.

I swallowed my urge to smirk and entered the foyer. "I don't really drink, but thank you."

The woman's shallow smile flipped upside down. "But King *said* I was to get you a drink."

If I didn't know any better, I'd say there was a sliver of fear buried beneath her insistence. Otherwise, why would her panties be wadding up simply because I'd refused a cocktail? *He owns her. He has to.* He was probably fucking her.

God, I hate you, King.

I felt my face turn a nice shade of pissy red. "King can go fuck himself," I said in the sweetest voice possible, "which I will personally let him know if you show me to him."

She raised her dark brows and gestured toward a long hallway to the left.

I gave her a cordial nod and followed along, trying not to notice the perfect lines of her waist and hips.

I quickly shoved my jealousy down a deep dark hole ideal for storing emotions that no longer served me or would only lead to self-pity. I refused to be *that* woman. I refused to feel lesser or weak because he'd left me. *He* was the weak one, the flawed one, the man who made promises he didn't keep. Me? I'd fought like hell to do right by him. I *had* done right by him.

We passed several closed doors, and the eerie silence crept into my ears like venomous spiders.

"Where is everyone?" I asked.

The woman turned the corner and stopped in front of a narrow closet door. "Right this way." She pushed it open to reveal a dimly lit staircase with another door at the bottom.

Fuck. That's the basement. I suddenly would've given everything to have my Seer abilities back.

They might tell me what I was in for. On the other hand, maybe it was for the best. I couldn't let fear get in my way and there couldn't be anything happy-shiny down there.

"Thank you." I stepped past her and gripped the cold iron railing with my clammy hand, taking care not to lose my footing or catch my hem with my heels.

Fuck me. This sucks. I forced my shaky legs to descend the staircase. When I reached the bottom, I paused with my hand on the handle, hearing rhythmic murmuring through the door, like a person praying or chanting. *Or holding a séance?*

Well, that's not at all fucking horrifying. I really wished I could've taken that stiff drink. And worn pants. Much easier to run away in. Because whatever King was up to, it couldn't be good. To my knowledge, King didn't normally sit around trying to converse with the dead. He *was* the dead. Or he had been and then he wasn't and now he was once more?

Shit. I have no clue. But the point was that most souls bound to this world, due to strong emotional ties, curses, or whatever, didn't generally walk around interacting with the living and investing money or flying in private jets. King was special. He'd refused to let a little thing like death get in his way. He'd spent thousands of years seeking out ways to pass himself off as the living. Once he got that down, he realized he needed help to achieve his ultimate goal and started 10 Club. I supposed it was genius. He put his supernatural talents to work, doing favors for club members: killing people's enemies, hunting down lost or stolen items. In return, 10 Club members begged, borrowed, and stole things he wanted or needed, like a giant evil swap meet for really crazy rich people. His end game, though, was finding a way back into a living breathing body and to end his pain. And he had. But it was with my help. Not 10 Club's.

Only he tossed it all away for Mack.

So now the question begged, what was King doing behind this basement door? I slowly turned the handle and pushed open the creaky wooden door. "Holy shit."

CHAPTER FOUR

"Nice of you to fucking join us, Ms. Turner," said King, while I locked my knees to keep them from buckling. "By the lack of punctuality, I am guessing you don't actually want to find that wayward husband of yours."

Oh, shit. Be strong, Mia. Be strong. My body twitched with the urge to run, but my brain said stay. I wanted to know what the hell King was doing. It might explain why he'd come back from the dead a second time.

I took a small step inside the basement, which reeked of incense and the coppery aroma of fresh blood. I could only assume it came from the dripping red symbols painted on the cement walls and floor. Or perhaps it came from the crimson mess on King's crisp, once-white tuxedo shirt.

I don't think it's coming from those guys. Five elegantly dressed people, two women and three men, lay on the floor, their bodies stretched out, face up, with the tops of their heads touching to form what looked like wheel spokes. They seemed to be the only items in the basement not covered in blood, but they looked dead.

"What the hell is-is going on?" I spoke softly.

"What the hell does it look like?" His steely gray eyes stuck to my face like an angry lion ready to pounce.

"It-it looks like you killed your dinner guests?" I stepped back, now wondering if he'd intended for me to be the sixth spoke in the body wheel.

Before I could utter another word, King materialized in front of me and grabbed my wrist. I shrieked and tried to pull back, but his grip felt like shards of glass crawling through my veins. It was him. He was inside me, trying to dig around inside my head. He'd done it before and there was little I could do to fight, except for—

I lifted my knee and struck him straight in the groin. He let out a grunt, releasing me and doubling over. *I guess he can still feel pain. Lucky me.*

I turned and bolted for the stairs, my shoes making it impossible to climb as fast as I wanted or needed. Halfway up, my right heel snagged the hem of my dress, launching my body forward. *Fuck!* I caught the railing with one hand, but my weight sent me swinging sideways. Part of my back and shoulder slammed into the plaster wall with a thud. I grunted and felt the railing sliding right from my hand, followed by my body launching sideways down the stairs in a twisted dive. I knew the moment I landed, the pain would follow. No, I didn't mean the ungraceful touchdown on the cold basement floor. I meant King would show no mercy.

My body hit the bottom step at an awkward angle, driving the sharp corners into my rib and hip. I extended my arm to break the fall and felt my wrist bend at a weird angle. I wailed and sort of bounced down the rest of the way, my face landing next to King's shiny black dress shoes.

He flipped me onto my back and glared down with those pale gray eyes, his jaw ticking away. I knew it was over for me. Mack had been right. I shouldn't have come.

Without a word, he reached for my arm.

"Wait! Please don't kill me. We have a ba—"

He seemed possessed as he grabbed my throbbing wrist and pulled a small blade from his coat pocket.

Oh, shit. This nightmare just kept getting worse. "King, stop! Fucking let me g—"

He sliced.

I screamed, half out of pain, half out of fear. What the fuck was he doing?

With fingers of blood trickling down my arm, he dragged me across the room toward the other dinner guests. He reached for something on the floor, and I realized it was a small metal wineglass that reminded me of the ones used for drinking port, with a stem and flute shape.

"Stop! What are you doing?" I whimpered.

He scraped the lip of the cup up my arm to collect the blood.

"Motherfuckingpsycho! Let me the hell go—"

"Silence, Ms. Turner," he said calmly. "You are making this much more difficult than necessary, and my patience with you wore out ten minutes ago."

Ten minutes ago, I'd been in my rental car, on my way here, late by a few minutes. It was so very King to be out of patience before his patience ever began. Not that it mattered in this moment.

King dropped my arm and turned away from me, stepping into the human circle, where he placed the cup. I started to crawl away, dragging my dress across the sticky cement floor, trying not to think about my wrist or the dripping gash.

King began to recite a long string of words that fused together inside my mind, making them impossible to decipher. Within moments, the air began to whip from every direction, my curls lashing at my face. I felt the room spinning, and then just like that, the room fell dark.

CHAPTER FIVE

"Ms. Turner?" My body lying over a soft surface, I felt a warm hand stroke my cheek and heard King's hypnotically deep voice cut right through me, rubbing intimately against my thoughts. My body stirred with delight, triggering a soft groan.

Oh, how I missed that, the feeling of closeness we once had. I suppose I sensed our connection from the first moment we met, but after I'd brought him back to life and ended his torment, it definitely became stronger.

Nevertheless, our bond had always gone beyond the physical and emotional. It went beyond man and woman in love. It felt as though our souls had been forged from the same fiery heart that refused to be pulled apart. Sometimes, I felt our connection most when we lay in bed, barely awake, the world quiet around us. With my eyes closed, I'd listen to his soft deep breaths, feel the warmth of his body on the sheets beside me, and I knew in my heart that he breathed because of me, he lived for me. Sometimes I felt the depths of our connection after he'd made hard, hot love to me. His large body draped over mine, he would breathe into my ear and whisper, "I love you, Mia. I love you more than life itself." "I love you, too," I would say, wondering how life could be so cruel, yet ultimately lead to such a beautiful place. I was the woman who'd won the heart of an enigma, a powerful king who refused to rest until he found a way for us to truly be together, even if it had meant living through three thousand years of hell.

Our love wasn't a fairytale. It was epic and im- possible. Yet…there we were.

However, our time of bliss would be short-lived. Less than a year. The last time we'd been together, King had been frantic, trying to keep Mack from ending his own life. Mack, too, had suffered from a breed of curses that made his existence a living hell. Death was supposed to be his only way out. "I can't live without him, Mia. I just don't know how," King had said, nearly pushed to tears. At the time, I understood Mack had been King's only reminder of a time when he'd been alive and good. But I never thought King would trade me for his brother even if I loved King so much that I would've never asked. Because that was the funny thing about love; you wanted what was best for the people who owned your heart. You truly did. Yet, at the same time, there was a pettiness to love, because when you were not chosen above all others, a tiny piece of your heart couldn't help but feel a little broken. *Why was my happiness not more important to him? Why wasn't our son more important to him?* Archon was only three months old, for fuck's sake. Hadn't that meant something to King?

"Ms. Turner, it is time for you to wake now." King's hypnotically masculine voice burrowed into my skull. He was digging around again. I hated that he could do that. "Tell me, who is this child of yours."

Crap. I had purposefully avoided thinking of Arch. I didn't want King knowing about him. *Safer that way.*

My eyelids peeled apart. "Stay out of my head, King," I mumbled, noticing that he'd bandaged my wrist.

"Afraid that is not my style, Ms. Turner." He smiled at me—just for a moment—but from what I could see, it was genuine. And it made my heart pump equal parts of sadness and joy. No one in this world could ever make me feel like he did when he smiled.

Fuck, Mia. What's wrong with you?

I threw up a mental wall between us. I might have lost my Seer abilities, but I still knew how to close off my emotions. Of course, King could simply decide to go scratching around inside my brain again, so I offered something to satisfy him.

"My child is dead," I lied. "Complications."

"A shame, to be sure." He narrowed his penetrating gray eyes. "Am I to assume this is why your husband vanished?"

"No. My husband loved us."

"So you believe there was foul play."

I looked away, my eyes scanning the small guest room with light gray curtains, white carpet, and a dark painting of a demon dancing with a cherub around a fire. A tall dresser in the corner had a bottle of scotch—my favorite—set out on a silver tray with two glasses.

"I think he left of his own free will," I muttered.

"You simply do not know why."

I nodded yes.

"Well." King stood and slid his hands into the pockets of his black slacks. His shirt was still a bloody mess. "In my experience, these things generally come down to another woman or—"

"No." My head snapped in his direction. "He wouldn't do that."

"Or," he continued, "you simply weren't enough for him."

"Fuck you." My eyes narrowed. "What the hell would you know about *enough*?"

"Nothing you might consider as a credential." He dipped his head of thick black hair. "Now, if you'll excuse me, Ms. Turner, I must get changed and attend to my guests."

"You mean the ones you murdered in the basement? And where do you get off cutting me, you piece-of-shit barbarian?" My hands began to tremble as the fresh memories snapped back into my head.

He laughed. "I assure you they are alive and well. Thanks to your blood," he added. "If you care to see for yourself, you may come down and join us for the party."

Sure. Every girl wants to mix, mingle, and snack after being assaulted by her evil dead husband. Dreamy as hell. "Yippy. Be right down," I sneered.

He tsked and slowly shook his head. "Then stay here if you like. But, Ms. Turner, do not leave this house. You are to remain here with me."

I laughed. "I don't think so."

"Do not push me, woman, or I may be forced to take another look inside that complicated head of yours and discover where your not-so-dead son is and invite him to stay with me."

He knows I lied about Arch. My nostrils flared and my rage exploded like an underwater bomb—not a lot of noise, but the ripples were deadly nonetheless. Nobody threatened my baby. *Our* baby.

"I'll kill you before I ever let you touch him," I said in a controlled voice.

King turned to leave. "Let me know if your wrist gives you any issues." He reached for the door handle. "I know a Seer who has the gift of healing. I'm sure she'll come if I ask."

I held back a gasp. *Fucking bastard.* That woman with the gift of healing was the only other Seer in existence I knew of: Theodora—aka, Teddi, Mack's soon-to-be wife. She was a good woman who'd suffered enough. And I highly doubted that King would ask. Nuh-uh. He would threaten.

I lifted my chin. "I'll manage."

"Then I shall see you downstairs. I will send Meledia to help you into a new dress." He left the room, and the chill left with him.

Asshole. Now he'd crossed the line. He'd hurt me and threatened our child and Teddi. Mack had been right. King had to die as quickly as possible. *Because that man is no longer my husband.*

I would have to get closer and wait for the right moment.

༺ ༻

Now wearing strappy black heels and a backless black dress that King "just happened to have lying around," I descended the staircase from the second floor and followed the voices. This time, the house buzzed with life. No. Not a fucking joke. Joy, laughter, and glasses clanking.

I stopped at the base of the stairs to the side of the foyer, my hand white-knuckled around the butt of the railing.

What the fuck is going on? One minute I'm living through a scene straight from the *Exorcist* and the next I'm listening to the celebratory sounds of mingling?

"Ms. Turner, very nice of you to join us. Don't you look lovely." King appeared a few feet away and held out his strong hand. My body lit up. He looked like a fairytale prince—tall, imposing, and unfathomably handsome in a fresh tuxedo.

God. And those lips. So blatantly sensual. They were the sort of lips a woman looked at and just knew he could kiss and suck and—

I mentally elbowed myself and straightened my spine. *Stay focused, Mia.* That beautiful face, with the proud cheekbones and square jaw covered in black stubble, was just a façade. Underneath was the devil, cruel and heartless.

The pain too much in my bandaged right arm, I extended the left. King showed no sympathy for my wounds and escorted me into the party being held in the large living room with gleaming hardwood floors and modern white furniture. There was a full bar in one corner and a piano in the other, where a woman played soft jazz. A set of open French doors led out to an empty torchlit terrace. It seemed everyone wanted to be inside, toasting, talking, smiling.

I couldn't digest. Five of these twenty people had been front and center in the satanic circle of doom earlier this evening. Now they snacked on appetizers and sipped champagne?

"Don't look so surprised, Ms. Turner. I told you they were alive."

But…but… "So what was all that in the base-ment?"

His silvery eyes twinkled with smugness. "It

doesn't concern you." He grabbed my elbow and shuffled me to the corner of the room, directly in front of the piano, where he pulled me against his warm hard body.

"What are you doing?" I protested quietly. I knew better than to make a scene at a 10 Club party, which was what this was. It had to be.

"We're dancing." He flashed his trademark charming smile.

I ignored his powerful heartbeat and how he seemed like anything but dead. I ignored the vibrant look in his eyes and the pink tint to his olive cheeks. I couldn't allow myself to think about how he used to hold me and how it made me feel naked from the inside out. He was once my drug.

"You didn't answer my question," I said.

He smirked, but didn't speak.

"My wrist is sprained," I said. "You cut me and used my blood. I'm fairly sure this involves me."

"Concern and involvement are two distinct things, Ms. Turner. I suspect a Seer knows the difference." His body swayed, and he forced me to move with him. His grip around the base of my back felt tighter than a pair of handcuffs.

"I'm not a Seer." *Not anymore.* Of course, my husband, the real King, knew that.

"Do you take me for an idiot?"

"I gave up my Seer gifts in exchange for my life, which is something you couldn't possibly know. But yes, I think you're an idiot."

King loosened his grip and chuckled. "Touché. So am I to guess that your *husband* had something to do with you losing your Seer abilities?" He spat the word *husband* like it was the name of his worst enemy.

"Why do you care?"

"I care about many things."

"No. *You* are a heartless monster," I pointed out.

"A monster who can help you get what you want as long as you appease him."

"By appease do you mean you'd like to bleed me out?"

He shook his head but maintained that wickedly charming smile. Or was it just wicked? "How you push me, Ms. Turner. It is as if you have a death wish."

"I'm standing here dancing with you, so maybe I do."

"Because of him? This pathetic excuse of a man who left you with a void in your life and a broken heart?" He lowered his head and whispered into my ear, "I can make you feel special again, Mia. I can give you a life without worries or pain. I can take care of your every need."

What? He can't be serious. Not that he could understand the irony of the situation, but at the very least he had to know that hitting on me was ludicrous given what he'd just put me through. But that was King. Bold, sure of himself, fearless. That was what made him so irresistible to women.

Luckily for me, I knew exactly how easy it was to be seduced by his powerful presence and dangerous beauty.

"No, thanks. I can take care of my own needs." I flashed a tight little smile.

His eyes narrowed. He didn't like being shot down. "Very well. If you are happy with your lot in life…"

I looked up at him. "To the contrary, King. I couldn't be more unhappy. I think it's a sad, sad thing—a man who breaks his vows. I think you call those sorts of people welshers. I call them pathetic."

He laughed into the air with eyelids pinched, his deep, deep voice ricocheting off the walls.

"What the hell is so funny?" I snarled.

He looked down at me and resumed his swaying. "I find your gritty attitude refreshing."

"There is nothing refreshing about loving someone and sacrificing your own flesh and blood to help him, only to be betrayed."

King's snide grin faded from his face, and he stopped moving. His eyes glazed over, and he suddenly seemed off in another place.

Is he remembering something? I hoped so. I hoped he'd snap out of whatever had taken a hold of him and made him forget me.

"King? There is an urgent call for you," said a soft, submissive voice to our side.

I looked to find Meledia, the woman who'd answered the door earlier.

He quickly snapped to. "Who is it?"

She nervously glanced at me and then back at him. "Your brother."

"What does that fucker want?" he growled.

"He wouldn't say, sir. Only that it was important."

King hesitated for a moment. "Tell him I will be there in a minute." He glanced down at me and was about to say something, but stopped and just stared.

"Yes?"

He placed his hand on my cheek, and though I knew he wasn't made of flesh and blood, the warmth still felt real. "I think I once loved a woman like you."

My heart jolted inside my rib cage. He *was* remembering.

"What happened to her?"

"I think she misunderstood me." He turned and left the room, leaving me standing there with his guests giving me side glances.

What the hell did that mean? Yes, he *had* to be remembering, but what had I—the woman he loved once—misunderstood? Because I'd fucking love to know before I helped kill him.

CHAPTER SIX

Despite the pain in my arm, I decided to stick around and do a little mingling instead of leaving the party. Two reasons: One, I wanted to find out what had just happened in that basement. It could affect how we dealt with ending 10 Club. And two, I wanted King to see me walk out that front door. I knew that defying him was a dangerous move, but now I knew he needed me—or at least my blood—and I wanted to keep the ball in my court, not his. King liked a challenge, and the bigger the hurdle, the more enticing. If he saw me as unattainable, it would only strengthen his resolve to own me. He would pursue, waiting for the right moment to strike. What he didn't know was that I was playing his game, waiting for my own moment, which meant getting close enough to gain access to that warehouse. *Lot ninety-four.*

Damn. How did my life end up being such a back-stabbing mess? I was like the poster child for drama.

For example, when King and I first met, it had been a time in my life when everything was in ruins.

My brother, Justin, an archeologist who'd been working in Southern Mexico, had gone missing, and I was doing everything I could to find him. Not only for me, but for my poor heartbroken parents, who still lived not far from here. However, every door I knocked on seeking help had been slammed in my face. No one cared if Justin had been taken. Not the embassy, not the local authorities, no one. Then a random woman told me about King—the man who could find anything or anyone for a price, so I went to see him. He had no issues offering help—aka taking advantage of my desperation—and steamrolling over my life.

This time had to be different.

There were people I cared about and needed to protect from this dangerous world. Thankfully, our son, Archon, was safe at home in a modern-day fortress King had built for us in Crete. King had personally warded the entire estate to keep anything "bad" away. He told me that not even his past could cross the property lines. I'd laughed at the time but now wondered if maybe King knew something was going to happen. After all, when it came to King, he was like a master chess player, able to see the outcome long before everyone else. Either way, I missed Arch, who was safer at home with the nanny, but I had to finish this. King had to die and stay dead. I just had to keep reminding myself that this evil man was not my husband.

I walked up to the bar and ordered a glass of

wine from Jeff—his name according to the badge on his red vest. As Jeff poured, a man came up and ordered a scotch, neat. I recognized him from the basement.

"Hi, nice party," I said, hoping I could find out something.

The man glanced at me and nodded, but didn't speak.

"So friendly," I muttered under my breath. Perhaps this man, "the human spoke," didn't like talking to strangers.

I turned my attention back to Jeff, who placed my wine in front of me over a cocktail napkin and then proceeded to pour vodka into a martini shaker for the man. *Not good.* He'd asked for a scotch.

Figuring that the bartender was King's property, and not wanting him to rub a 10 Club member the wrong way—generally a lethal move—I intervened.

"You can do the *martini* after you serve the gentleman *his scotch.* Neat," I added, jerking my eyes at the man, hoping Jeff would get the hint.

Jeff gave me a quick look but caught on. "As you like, ma'am." Jeff served the correct drink, thanks to me, and the gentleman went back to mingling without giving either of us another glance.

Jeff leaned in. "Thank you. I had no idea what he ordered. I just took a stab."

That's odd. "You didn't hear him say scotch?"

Jeff shook his head. "Not in English."

I was about to speak when my brain made an

inaudible click. My eyes gravitated to a tattoo on my left wrist. I'd had it for over a year now and barely thought about it anymore, but it was truly an incredible tattoo. Not for the artwork—really just an infinity shape—but because it had been given to me by another Seer, Hagne. She was long dead and had been a truly evil person, but the power in the ink was not. It allowed me to understand and speak any language.

"Was he speaking English earlier?" I asked.

Jeff bobbed his head. "Yeah, he ordered a vodka martini."

"In English."

"Yes," he confirmed.

What the hell was going on?

"Thanks." I took my glass and made my way out through the French doors onto the torchlit terrace. *Wow.* I took in the strings of lights hung around the edge of the yard, the candlelit tables with white linens, and an ice sculpture with a big "10C." I had to admit, King had gone all out to make this look like a real 10 Club event rather than a satanic ritual.

I slid my phone from my red satin evening bag and called Mack. It went straight to his voicemail.

Shit. That's right. He's talking to King.

"Mack," I said after the tone, "it's Mia. I saw King performing some ritual in his basement. There were five people lying on the floor and a chalice he filled with blood. My blood. Now they're all chitchatting and sipping drinks like nothing ever happ—"

"There you are, Ms. Turner." King's menacing voice came from behind me.

I froze. *Dang it.* "Gotta go." I ended the call and turned toward King, who still looked like his usual stunning self. "I was just checking in with a friend. And I'm afraid I have to go."

King's hostile expression turned downright lethal—lips tight, jaw clenched, brows frowning. "I think you are mistaken."

I chuckled and shook my head at my feet. "Oh, King. I love that you think you own me. But that wasn't the deal, remember?" I smiled up at him defiantly, using everything I had to mask any fear. He could kill me with the snap of his fingers if he liked. "Or are you a welsher, King? Because I seem to recall our arrangement being my ring in exchange for you finding my husband, which you haven't done yet."

He stared with those stunning, predatory eyes. "Right you are, Ms. Turner. And since I am a man of my word," he stepped aside, "you are free to leave."

I grinned like a smug bitch, but still dipped my head in gratitude. "Have a good night, King. Call me when you're ready to get serious about completing our transaction." I walked by him and grazed his arm. A familiar warmth shot through my entire body, sparking a deeper heat down to my core. It was as if my body craved him, needed him. I didn't want to feel like that. Not for him. But I did, and I had just done a piss-poor job of hiding my emotions.

Crap. Big mistake.

King grabbed my arm and whipped me back. My body slammed right into him, eliciting a gasp.

"Who the fuck are you?" he growled, holding me firmly by the shoulders.

He felt it, too. Oh God. That meant some part of him had to remember me.

I blinked up at him, trying not to notice the heat of his strong male body forged from pure will—his iron, unbendable will.

"I'm not sure I know what you mean," I said all too innocently.

His eyes twitching with equal parts irritation and anger, he said, "Don't fuck with me, Ms. Turner, because I will kill you."

"I'm not interested in fucking with you, King. I just want to find my husband." I cracked open the door inside my head and allowed my emotions to trickle out. I wanted him to feel the honesty in my words.

"No," he snapped, his deep voice filled with menace. "You're up to something. I can sense it."

Just then I felt ice-cold razorblades slicing through my veins and King pouring himself into my mind. I grunted in agony, trying to fight him, but I knew it was no use. This was one ability he had that

I had no skills to fight.

Suddenly, I saw him and me standing hand in hand on the beach, the warm white sand beneath our bare feet and the turquoise blues of the Mediterranean stretching as far as the eye could see. King's long black hair flitted with a gust of wind and his bare chest swelled with sleek muscles beneath deep olive skin. His lively eyes, a shocking shade of vivid blue, were like the waters of Crete he so much loved.

No. I don't want to see this. My heart exploded with a soul-crushing ache. This was the memory of a moment when my life changed forever—when King was alive, before curses, deaths, or any of that. I had unknowingly used my Seer abilities to go to him and traveled back over three thousand years. At first I'd thought I'd gone mad or died, but little by little, I had realized that it had been real. I had been wishing with every spark of life in my heart to *see* him as he once was, and my gifts delivered me. What I'd found wasn't a sadistic billionaire walking on the edge of sanity, searching for salvation, but a powerful king who deeply loved his people and would do anything for them. He served and protected them, and they worshipped him like a god. His beauty as a person reached beyond words. That was the moment I realized I loved him and always would.

"What the fuck is this?" King gave me a hard shake, jarring me from my hypnotic state.

I blinked away my tears and pushed back my tender thoughts. He could scratch around all he liked, but I would never let him inside my heart. Not again.

"I don't know what you're talking about," I said through tight lips.

He shook me again, making my teeth clack. "What witchery is this?"

"Witchery?" I coughed out a snide chuckle. For once, King sounded his age. "I don't know what you mean," I lied. "Maybe what you're seeing is a result of secret longings from your subconscious mind."

He snarled sadistically. "You and I standing on a beach, holding hands? Fucking doubtful, Ms. Turner."

"Or maybe you dream of having long flowing hair. But who am I to judge?"

"Think you're funny, Ms. Turner? Let's see how much you laugh when I strip the soul from your body and offer it up to a few of my friends who get off on breaking little girls like you."

I wasn't afraid of 10 Club. I was only afraid of who I had to become in order to fight them. I'd crossed that line once, and it was enough to make me realize that a person could only cross it so many times before they couldn't come back.

"Sorry, King. But you scare me about as much as a bad burrito. Might feel uncomfortable for a little while, but I've survived worse."

"My, how you have a way with words, Ms.

Turner. Let's see what you have to say in my basement." He yanked on my right arm and the pain shot into my shoulder.

I swallowed every ounce like a bitter pill, refusing to give him any satisfaction. I would never bow or shrivel. Not to him.

I snapped away my screaming arm. "I have a way with don't *fuck* with me, so back the hell off unless you want your balls kissed by my knee again."

He shook his head. "I will never understand the colloquialisms of today. Crassness elevated to the Neanderthal era."

I pointed my finger in his face. "The next time you hurt me, cut me, or lie to me, King, my colloquialisms will be the least of your worries. You'll wish you'd stayed dead."

He gave me a look, and I realized my epic error.

Shit. My blood pressure leaked through my black heels into the cement below. *Stupid, stupid, Mia.* I wasn't supposed to know he was dead. It would require one of two things: I either had Seer abilities, which allowed me to see his "true colors," or I knew more about him than I'd let on.

Fuck, fuck, fuck. Nobody knows anything about him besides me and Mack. Okay, and a few of King's most trusted bodyguards. But in King's mind, I didn't exist, so he would think I'd been sent by his brother, and it was paramount that he didn't suspect Mack of anything. I could misdirect him and blame one of King's bodyguards, but he'd kill them.

"I've been trying to get my Seer abilities back," I lied. "The best I can manage is a flicker here and there." A complete pile of bullcrap. I would never be getting them back. The ancient Seers had taken them from me in exchange for my life after I'd been stabbed by one of King's psychotic bodyguards who had a thing against me. Like I said, my history with King was a long and complicated one.

King's hand lunged for my throat and squeezed, his beautiful face a tangle of frightening snarls. "Now I know you're lying."

"You don't know shit," I croaked.

"What game are you playing?" he growled.

"No games. I want to know what happened to my husband. I want to know why he left."

He tilted his head, studying my face with intensity, and then snapped his hand away.

I stumbled back, pressing my shaking hand to my neck.

King winced and ground the heels of his hands against his tightly shut eyes. What was happening to him?

"Tell me," he grumbled, "where is the last place you saw your husband?"

King didn't do or say anything without a reason, so I hoped he asked because he remembered something. I couldn't lie; I wanted answers before Mack and I twisted the proverbial knife in his back.

"Crete," I said.

He removed his hands from his handsome face,

and I noticed dark circles under his eyes. Very unusual for a ghost who literally willed himself into existence. "Is this where you live?"

"I'm from here—San Francisco—but yes. I live in Crete now." *In a beautiful home you built for us. We were supposed to grow old together there.*

His gray eyes locked onto my face. I'm sure he found it suspicious that I lived on the island where he was born. "Well, then, take me to the last spot you saw him."

"Greece is pretty far." And nowhere near his warehouse here in San Francisco, which I still needed to find a way into. *Lot ninety-four.*

"Thank you for pointing that out, Ms.—"

"If you'll let me finish; I was about to say that I don't think he's there, so the trip would be a waste of time." *You're here. Right here with me, King.*

"I appreciate your concern for the efficient use of my time; however, I am a big boy. A very ancient one, but you already knew that, didn't you?"

"Yes." I bobbed my head, wanting to buy a few moments to think. If we went to Greece, he'd be closer to Archon, our little baby. King was volatile and dangerous, and frankly, I had no idea what King might do with our son if they met. Arch had my Seer blood running through him, and though, to the best of my knowledge, the gene only expressed itself in particular women, that didn't mean our son had no value. Seers were nearly extinct, and our son would be capable of carrying that bloodline forward someday. 10 Club members would love to get their hands on little Arch.

My stomach tightened with the thought. On the other hand, Greece was where King had been born and where his people died. It was the place he first met me. Going might jar his memory. And King himself had warded the property. No one bad could get anywhere near the home. That included himself, I assumed.

This was a difficult call. *Maybe I should keep pushing him to remember. Here in San Francisco.*

"Ms. Turner, you seem to have gone somewhere interesting inside that head of yours. Shall I join you?" He crossed his arms over his chest, looking like the domineering, ancient king he once was, despite his elegant tuxedo.

"No." I glared up at King. "I think you need to stop wasting my time and do what you promised."

He chuckled sadistically. "I am wounded, Ms. Turner. Are you not enjoying your time with me?"

"No. And time is running out. We have to find him."

"Why the urgency?"

Because Mack plans to kill you one way or the other. And I needed to know the truth before it was too late.

"In your own words? That's not your concern."

"Let's get this straight, Ms. Turner. Everything pertaining to you from this point forward concerns me."

"Because of my blood?" I raised a brow.

He stared into my eyes for a moment and then his gaze fell to my lips. I wanted it to mean something more than he simply found me fuckable. I wanted it to mean he knew my lips and dreamed of them like I dreamed of his mouth—the way it once moved over my neck and nipples, the way his lips used to brush against my earlobes when he made love to me. But his lips also reminded me of the happiest times of my life. I used to love the way his lips curled more on the right side when he laughed with joy, like the day I told him I was pregnant. I don't think I'd ever seen him so happy. He literally didn't stop smiling for a week. Merely looking at those lips reminded me of the sweet words he'd said when I was in labor for twenty-two hours, going out of my mind with pain and fear. I couldn't go on another minute. "Cut him out. Please. I can't do it."

"Mia, you're almost there," he'd said, brushing back the sweat-soaked strands of hair from my forehead. "You can do this," he'd leaned forward and whispered in my ear. "You're the strongest woman I've ever known. You brought me back from the dead and gave me life again. *This* is much easier. *This* you can do." He placed a soft kiss with those lips on my cheek and pressed his forehead to mine. "Now push," he'd said softly and took my hand. Archon came out two minutes later, and King never once let go of my hand. Not until he got to hold the baby. Then he'd been speechless. Literally speechless. Those sweet lips simply curled into that lopsided smile again and made me forget what I'd just gone through. King's lips were my Achilles' heel.

As I stared at the painful reminder of the life we no longer had together, King suddenly glanced at the crowd inside his house and then back at me, his eyes narrowing.

Oh no. I knew that look. He was puzzling something out.

"What?" I asked.

"I'm simply wondering something."

"Yes?"

He scratched the black scruff on his jaw. "I'm wondering if this husband of yours is real. I find it odd that you are unwilling to go to Crete, where I might pick up his trail. And then there's the image I saw in your head of us holding hands on a beach."

"He is real, and I don't see your point."

"My point is that you're not telling me something." He stepped in closer. "What are you up to, Ms. Turner? I will find out one way or another."

Dammit. I had to earn his trust, but I knew trying to convince him with words would be fairly useless. Actions meant more to him.

"Okay, then." I sighed and walked past him, heading inside.

"Where are you going?"

"Call me when you get to Crete." I left his house but felt his eyes on me until I got to my car.

He definitely suspected me, but maybe Crete wasn't such a horrible idea. Maybe it was just what he needed to remember.

God, but Arch.

I mentally shook my head at myself as I started the engine. I'd been so eager, so angry and upset by what King had done to me that I'd wanted revenge. And then for about ten seconds I'd wanted closure. But now, all I wanted was for those I loved to never, ever have to worry about 10 Club.

Did I want King back, too? I couldn't lie. I missed him so much that I couldn't bear to think about it anymore. But I wouldn't get back what we'd had because nothing under the sun could explain away his choices.

Suddenly, part of me wondered if this was why he couldn't remember me. Maybe he'd done it on purpose, choosing to let us go forever. He had to know there'd be no turning back if he left us like he had—unprotected, devastated, and feeling betrayed.

Either way, I had to keep pushing forward. And at the moment, forward meant going to Crete.

CHAPTER SEVEN

I could hardly breathe on the long flight home to Greece. I felt far too nervous about seeing King again, and I missed Arch in a way that could only be described as a heartache. It wouldn't go away until I held him again.

Arriving at nine in the morning, I grabbed a cab home even though I could've called for our driver. I wasn't a fan of servants and bodyguards. That was King's world. Not mine. Same went for this home—a gleaming white modern mansion perched high on a hill overlooking the ocean, complete with tennis court, helicopter pad, fruit orchards and a private beach. King had spared no expense when he'd built it for us, using the excuse that this was the place we would live in the rest of our lives, so it had to be special.

I burst through the front door and sprinted through the formal living room, dining room and kitchen, looking for Arch and Ypirétria, the seventy-year-old nanny who acted more like a fifty-year-old.

"Hello?" I called out.

A faint little coo caught my attention, and I followed the sound through the kitchen into the backyard, which was really a large walled-in terrace overlooking the beach below. I spotted Arch in his little baby swing on the lawn, Ypirétria sitting in a chair next to him.

"Mommy's home."

Arch looked at me with his big blue eyes and flashed a toothless smile. For the first time in days, my heart felt full again.

"God, I missed you." I ran and scooped him up, covering him in kisses.

I spent the next day holding him as much as I could and trying to catch up on sleep. By the second day, I started to wonder what was taking King so long. I wanted this all to be over as quickly as possible. Worst of all, the time had finally given me a chance to digest the chaotic emotions I'd been bottling up. First, there was the grief of losing the love of my life. Then I'd found out that he'd volunteered to die so that Mack would live. I had cried so hard I threw up because I couldn't stomach the pain. And then Mack called with the news about King being back, and I threw some clothes in a suitcase. I told Ypirétria I would be back in a few days, and I hopped on a plane to San Francisco. Between King dying and seeing him alive again, I hadn't really had time to do much else other than react. Now I was beginning to see the pieces coming together and they told me that I needed to think through my next move carefully.

One, I still wanted King to remember me. I wanted to know why he'd made his choice or if he had some plan that had gone horribly wrong. If by some small chance he could be saved, I felt I owed it to myself and Arch.

Two, and a higher priority, 10 Club had to end. There were no ifs, ands, or buts. They were a constant threat to someone like me who had married a man with many 10 Club enemies, not to mention everyone wanted his arsenal in that warehouse back in San Francisco. He had everything from rare priceless art to the most frighteningly powerful objects. This was why King had made me a promise to dismantle the club. He knew it was a question of when, not if, they would come after me—a Seer who they believed had powers and access to King's wealth.

Three, Mack had to be dealt with somehow. No, I didn't mean in a shady mob kind of way. I would never hurt him or his beautiful fiancée, Teddi. Those two had gone through their own kind of hell to be together, and I wanted them to be happy and safe. I just needed Mack to give me a little more time. He clearly wasn't on board given that Teddi happened to be a Seer, too. The people in 10 Club would love to get their hands on someone like her, and with King not being himself, I'm guessing Mack knew his own brother might try to barter her away or use her in some manner like he'd used me.

So yeah, I couldn't blame Mack for wanting to take the 10 Club out ASAP.

Still, I needed to push forward and do what I could to find out what happened to King. That meant getting closer to him and pushing for answers.

On the third day, I had just put Arch down for a nap in the nursery—a beautiful room with a view of the ocean and murals of sea creatures—and went downstairs to start lunch. Ypirétria was doing her usual routine, which often involved yelling at me for trying to help fold clothes or clean up the kitchen. Housework was her domain and she was a very territorial creature. But her entire family had loyally served King for thousands of years, so that made her almost like a grandmother. I certainly couldn't do without her.

I opened the fridge, searching for something easy on my stomach, and my cell began to vibrate in my pocket.

Unknown caller.

I hit the green button on the tiny screen. "Hello?"

"Ms. Turner, so nice to hear your voice."

Game time. My heart filled with an unpleasant weight. "King, nice of you to finally call."

"Is that a note of sarcasm I detect?"

I blew out a breath. "Where are you?"

"Right outside. I would have come to your front

door, but it is the strangest thing," his voice became pissy all of a sudden, "seems that someone has warded your property. Quite well, in fact."

Yeah. You did. And I felt nothing but relief that King could not enter because he'd made sure nothing "bad" could get inside.

"A girl can never be too careful. I mean, there are all sorts of crazy people out there. Some of them even like to slice your wrists and steal your blood."

He laughed. "Are you always so amusing, Ms. Turner?"

"Only for you, King."

"Excellent. Bring your amusing ass outside. I have some pleasing topics to discuss."

"What kind of pleasing?" Could he have remembered something? My pulse accelerated.

"See you on the beach."

The call ended, and I rushed to find Ypirétria, who was folding Arch's clothes in the laundry room. I told her to stay put.

I changed into a pair of jeans and red sweater to shield me from the unusually cold January weather and headed out to the yard and through our gate that led to the steps and beach below. Off in the distance, I spotted King's impressive form—boxy shoulders, lean muscled frame, confident stance—in faded jeans and a dark sweater. My heart fluttered for a moment as I watched him standing there, gazing at something off on the horizon beyond the waves, just like I'd seen my King do a hundred times.

He was still so beautiful. *I miss you, King.*

I squared my shoulders and walked up beside him.

"Another beautiful day here on the island of Crete, is it not, Ms. Turner?" He didn't bother to look at me.

The wind surged against the front of our bodies, pushing back King's shiny black hair and making mine fly all over the place. I should've worn a ponytail, but there'd been no time for primping.

"It's wonderful," I said dryly. I had zero desire to talk about the weather. "So tell me, King, did you pick up my husband's trail?" *Do you remember who you are?*

"You haven't shown me the last place you saw him."

"We said goodbye at the front door."

He glanced sideways at me with an arched brow. "And where did he say he was going?"

"To help his brother."

"What sort of trouble was his brother in?"

Where is he going with this? "That I couldn't say," I lied, not wanting to give too much away.

King turned to me and shook his head, tsking. "You are a terrible liar, Ms. Turner. Now I suggest you come clean and tell me what you're up to, or today will be your last day on earth."

I would've shrugged him off—just another threat—but I knew this man. He wasn't joking.

"What happened to that pleasing news?" I asked.

"I did not say who would be pleased." He glanced at me and flashed a devilish smile.

So he'd just said that to lure me outside. I could make a run for the house, but King would have me in two seconds.

I sighed and rubbed my eyes with the heels of my palms. "I guess that means you don't need any more of my blood," I muttered.

"You have all I require, and bagged Seer juice will do just fine."

I guessed he didn't require a lot of "Seer juice" because I was about as powerful as a blank bullet. All pop, no power.

I dropped my arms. "So you actually came here to kill me?"

"That depends on you, Ms. Turner. Tell me the truth, and I might let you live. Lie to me, and I will end you right here, drain your blood, and dance in your memory at my dinner party tonight."

"You're having another party? Here?"

"Yes. I have a home not too far from here."

Wow. So King had another house I never even knew about.

I always accepted that King was a man of many secrets. I knew what I was getting into when I fell in love with him, but that didn't mean his secrets didn't bother me.

"It's quite old—been in my family for centuries."

"Sounds wonderful," I said flatly.

"It is. And it is entirely your choice if you wish to live to see it."

So this was it. I could come clean, or he would kill me. Not even a hundred yards from Arch's window and less than twenty feet from the spot where we first made love. King had built our luxurious fortress here for a reason. He always had one. Reasons, I mean.

I cleared my throat and brushed my wild hair from my eyes. "Well, I'm sure that you think you want the truth, but you and I both know that sometimes we really want something entirely different." I glanced toward the house. "For example, tell me what you see when you look at that house."

"I see a home that is built to look like a show palace when it is really a well-guarded stronghold. The walls are high enough to keep out people and prying eyes. The windows are tinted so no one can see in. There is a flat roof with a three-hundred-and-sixty-degree view of the area around the home, which makes it ideal for defense. And if I were to guess, there are several tunnels running under the home that lead under the main road, where there are smaller homes with garages, and that at least one of those homes is owned by you and your husband and contains cash, cars, and weapons."

I blinked, but didn't confirm. I mean, it was no

shock to me that King would guess his own defense plan.

He continued, "It is exactly the type of home I built for my wife."

My heart jolted against my rib cage. "What wife?" I grabbed his sleeve, my heart fluttering around in my stomach. "What wife, King?"

He pinched his brow and winced, seeming disoriented.

"King?" I should've been running, but I couldn't. "Look at me. Fucking look at me. Who do you see when you look at me, King?"

He finally looked, and all emotion drained from his face. "I see no one."

I snapped in that moment, and I knew I was snapping, but I'd kept so much bottled up that the thin scab just came right off.

Goddammit. Godfuckingdammit! "No." I slammed my fist into his chest. "Take another look. Look at that house. Look at my face." I reached into my pocket and held up my phone. There was a picture of me and King, both cradling Arch. "Look and fucking tell me what you see."

King's gray eyes stuck to the screen of my phone. The expression on his face—startle mixed with suspicion—made my hope bloom. *He remembers us.*

"Why are you and my brother holding that child?" he asked.

The bile nearly launched from my stomach.

"Your…*brother?*" I spat. "King, look at me. Please, I'm begging you."

"I am looking, and I am still waiting for a reply."

I grabbed the sides of his face, pushed myself up on my toes and kissed him hard. The heat passed through our lips into my body, overtaking me immediately. His tongue, so soft and silky, skilled and enticing, delved into my mouth and made me burn for him. Without thinking, I slid my arms around his tight waist and pressed my body into him, aching for the intense spark only we had.

He pushed me away and wiped his mouth with the back of his hand. "What the fuck, woman, are you doing?"

"I'm trying to make you see."

"What?"

"The truth." I reached for his hand and held it up to my lips as the tears leaked from my eyes. "I am your wife. That picture with the baby is you, not Mack." I looked up at him, hoping for a miracle. "I just want to know why you traded everything we had for death. You could've found another way to help Mack, but you just gave up so easily. Why, King? Tell me why you would do that to us."

A cleansing relief washed through me. My cards—raw, sad, and gritty—were out there on the table. So if there was a god, she would surely reward me with words of consolation from King—*It was all some big mistake. The devil made me do it. I was entranced by a 10 Club member.*

King pulled his hand away. "I cannot."

Cannot. "Cannot what?"

"I cannot allow you to continue with such treachery, Ms. Turner. I am afraid our journey ends here." His hand lunged for my throat, and his long fingers wrapped around my neck, squeezing with such force that I felt the bones in my neck bending.

I tried to push him away, but a man made of sheer will could not be deterred by anything physical in this world.

"Please," I croaked, "just let me go."

Vicious hatred simmered in his eyes. "You think you can mind-fuck me like that? You think you can stop me from taking 10 Club to the next level?"

I clawed at his hands, but it had no impact. "No," I croaked. "I just want to know why you swore to love me forever. But you welshed."

King's grasp loosened, but he didn't speak.

"We were everything to you. Can't you remember?" I whispered. "This house was built by you. Warded by you."

"Lies," he growled, grabbing my shoulders.

"No. Not lies, King." I placed my hand over my stomach, dreading what I was about to reveal but seeing no other way to get through to him. This little life inside me was so powerful that I could feel her from the moment she'd been conceived on the night King left. I'd been waiting to tell him when he came home. She was me and him and more powerful than I ever was. "Your daughter is here, and she needs you. But if you can't find a way back," I wiped away my tears, "then I have to protect her from you and those fucking evil people, King. She's too special."

King's nostrils flared and his gray eyes softened. "You are pregnant?"

Arch was three months old, and it was supposed to be near impossible to conceive so quickly, but I had. *Leave it to King to break every rule.*

I nodded. "She's yours."

"And so is that little boy," he stated.

I nodded again, feeling every muscle in my body coil with desperation. *Please, God. Please…*

"And someone has meddled with my mind to make me forget them."

"Yes," I whispered.

King looked away, his jaw pulsing, his lips flat, his fists clenched.

I waited with bated breath. Would he believe me or snap my neck?

Come on, King. Come on.

King swiveled toward me, snarling, and I shrank back.

Fuck. Fuck. I pushed out my hands, wanting to protect us from his wrath.

"I don't remember you, Mia. And I don't know who has fucked with my memory, but I promise that she," he looked at my stomach, "you, and my son will never have anything to fear. Not from me."

I'm not going to lie. His words were exactly what I wanted to hear. And I easily could've taken them at face value, but I was no longer that naïve young woman he'd first met, so desperate for help that she would put her faith in anyone who showed up with a little shiny armor. I had lost so much, and Arch and this baby needed me to play it smart. And don't think for a moment that I didn't catch the subtle meaning of those last words: "Not from me." That still left a whole hell of a lot of people to worry about.

"How do I know I can trust you?" I asked simply to see what he'd say.

"You don't." King slid a card from his jeans pocket. "Be here at eight o'clock. I would tell you not to be late, but I suspect it will do no good."

It wouldn't. "So it's another one of your dinner parties."

"Yes. And your blood will be required."

"Are you going to tell me what you're doing with it?"

"I am taking care of a threat that's long overdue."

Just like that, King disappeared into thin air.

Leaving me standing there staring at nothing.

CHAPTER EIGHT

What am I doing? I should just step away like Mack had said and let him deal with all this. That would be the safest move. But if I could find a way to get King back, didn't I owe it to all of us to try? No one walked away from the love of their lives just like that.

I checked my hair one last time in the vanity mirror of my private dressing room that was one of the many features King had added to the house, including a soaking tub smack in the middle of our enormous bedroom that opened up to a private balcony with a view of the ocean. The entire home reminded me of King's ancient palace here in Crete with its marble pillars and murals of ancient gods and sea creatures. I hated staying here without him. Too many memories.

It's not over yet, Mia. You still have one more shot.

Rallying my nerves, I applied a little hairspray to my straightened hair and finished applying a little smoky eye shadow. I looked as best as could be expected at a time like this.

"Mrs. Minos? The car is waiting when you're ready."

I glanced over my shoulder at the tall, thickly built man in his thirties, with dark wavy hair. Arno Spiros. Arno was one of King's most trusted bodyguards, but I didn't trust anyone with that last name. They were all loyal to King and only protected me because they'd been ordered to.

"Thank you, Arno. I'll be right down."

"Very good, ma'am."

He disappeared from the doorway, and I took one last look at myself in the mirror. My fitted dark blue dress hugged my curves and left little to the imagination. This was King's favorite dress. I'd only worn it once, and it had stayed on all of two minutes before he had me out of it. We ended up having takeout that night.

"Well, this is your last chance," I muttered to myself. Mack would soon come calling, and I couldn't necessarily argue with his plan. We all had so much to lose to 10 Club.

I passed by the nursery and kissed Arch goodbye before making my way downstairs to the waiting limo. Arno opened the car door with his usual steely professionalism. No eye contact.

I slid inside, and he took the driver's seat. Within moments we were headed down the main road, which skirted the coast. The sun had set hours ago, and I didn't like it. Bad things came out at night.

"I saw you on the security cameras with King

earlier," Arno said, breaking the silence, his eyes fixed to the curvy road. "I assume he has outsmarted death once again."

Arno didn't seem at all surprised.

"Yes. And you'll be happy to hear that he has completely forgotten me and Arch. He's also back to his old self." Meaning evil and basically a disembodied soul. "Maybe you'll get your king all to yourself again."

The Spiros had never liked the Seers and they certainly didn't like their king being married to one.

"I think you are mistaken about where our loyalties lie, Mrs. Minos."

I hated him calling me that. I hadn't changed my last name when I married King, whose official name was Draco Minos, the last king of ancient Minoa. However, getting petty about names wasn't going to get us anywhere.

"Where are your loyalties, Arno?"

"King relinquished his position before he left. We are loyal to you until Arch is grown."

Huh? This was slightly different than what King had told me.

"Are you saying that King isn't your king anymore?"

"Yes."

"So he…quit? And you decided not to tell me?"

King hadn't been a real king for a very long time, but in these people's eyes, he was and always would be their ruler. So I'd thought.

"Yes."

"When did this happen?" I asked.

"Before he died."

I looked out the window at the passing cars, pushing my tired mind to drill down. So King knew something was going to happen. He had to. It was one more piece of the puzzle that led me to believe King knew he would be taking a risk when he went to help Mack. And King never went in without some sort of plan.

If it's true, however, I'm on my own. King had no way of telling anyone what he'd thought might happen. He didn't remember. *Or if he does, he's not going to share it.*

Arno took a left and headed up a narrow road that cut through a hillside lined with olive trees.

"Did you know King had a second home here on the island?" I asked.

Arno glanced at me through the mirror. "King has many homes on Crete. He owns a lot of land."

I suppose that made sense. King had been around for a very long time.

A few minutes later, Arno turned again, pulling up to a two-story house with a stone façade. It looked like a historical home or museum with its perfectly restored stone exterior and wood-framed windows.

"How old is this place?" I asked.

"Over three hundred years, I am told."

Arno pulled the limo to a stop in front of the

gravel walkway.

"So practically brand new for King?" I said jok-ingly.

A black stretch limo pulled up behind us. Arno turned all the way around and looked me straight in the eyes. "Be careful tonight, Mia."

He'd made eye contact and used my first name, which meant he really wanted to make sure I listened. I didn't know whether to be grateful or just more nervous.

"Thank you. I will," I said.

Arno gave me a quick nod, slipped from the driver's seat, and came around to let me out. I took his hand and as gracefully as possible exited the vehicle.

"I will be waiting right over there." He glanced behind me toward the narrow road we'd taken here, where the chauffeurs were parking their cars to wait out the evening.

"I'll call when I'm ready to go," I said.

He dipped his head, and I headed for the arched doorway that led to a courtyard with a fountain. Surrounding the courtyard were two stories of plastered stone and a few wood-framed windows. Straight ahead was the front door with a stone arch, where King stood to the side in his elegant tuxedo, looking like a beautiful god greeting guests to Heaven.

My breath hitched and the back of my knees tingled with heat. The man always knew how to dress, how to look so goddamned handsome, even when he was about to make your life a living hell.

He spotted me from across the lit fountain, and I watched his fake smile transform into a wolfish gaze that made my chest knot. My body, especially those legs of mine, instinctually wanted me to go in the opposite direction. My heart, however, wanted something entirely different. It just wanted him. Deep. Hard. Now. The desire I felt for this man consumed me. It went beyond fucking and kissing and licking. He tugged every erotic thread running deep inside my being.

I pushed through my messy feelings and pasted on a smile, my eyes locked with his as I approached the front step.

"Ms. Turner," he dipped his head of thick black hair, "you look...ravishing," he said, his voice filled with sexual innuendo. His jaw bore its usual thick dark stubble I often loved to stroke with the tips of my fingers, and his lips had the devilish smile he always used on me when he wanted something.

I pretended not to notice.

"Thank you. You look very nice, too," I said.

Just then a busty blonde woman, same height and shaped face as me, came up with a snide grin and sexual hunger in her eyes. She wore a bright red dress cut so low that it almost showed her nipples.

"Sorry I took so long," she said with an annoyingly high-pitched voice. "Some fucking cunt was hogging the bathroom."

King took her hand. "You didn't miss much, my love. I was merely greeting our guests."

My...love? What the fuck? I couldn't believe my eyes or ears. He had another woman? *This woman?* But before I had a chance to process the major blow, he continued, "Hagne, may I introduce Mia Turner."

Hagne? My body went numb, yet I still managed to somehow step back in horror. "It's not possible." I shook my head from side to side, only vaguely aware of my phone ringing inside my evening bag.

Hagne cackled. "Nice to see you again, Mia."

But Hagne is dead. King beheaded her thousands of years ago. *And she's a fucking psycho.* I turned, intending to run like hell.

King inconveniently appeared in front of me, slipping his arm around my waist and pulling me into his hard body. "Just where do you think you're going?" His lips flickered with a carnal grin.

"To hell." Or maybe I was already there.

∽ ∾

King threw me into his library filled with wall-to-wall books and a leather reading chair—no phone—and then locked the door, but not before taking my handbag. I assumed he didn't want me calling anyone and interfering with his plans—whatever the hell those were. But make no mistake, every bone in my body shook with rage. If King had brought back Hagne, it was because he no longer cared for my safety one little bit.

Now I know why he said that he wouldn't harm me. Because Hagne sure the hell would. Three thousand years ago, she had been a powerful Seer, offered as a bride to King by her family, who had significant influence on the island. A marriage with a Seer would have served both families well, but Hagne had had a thing for Mack. And she was certifiably Cracker-Jack-crazy, coated in a thick layer of nuts with a psycho prize on the inside. I'd read her journal—King had kept it—which was how I knew she'd planned to use her Seer gifts to seduce Mack and then have him kill King so that Mack would be ruler. All that went sideways when I showed up and tried to stop her, for which she tried to kill me. King executed her, which almost started a war between himself and the Seers. To keep the peace and prevent his people from dying, King sacrificed his life—justice for Hagne's family. But King's death did little to change history. War still broke out. The Minoans still disappeared off the face of the planet, King's soul still ended up cursed, Mack still died and ended up cursed, and both brothers lived in torment for thousands of years, committing acts that haunted them. My attempted intervention had only restarted the entire story, just with different catalysts. Thankfully, Mack was eventually saved by Teddi, and King's torment ended with me bringing him back to life. *That's how it was supposed to end.* Now we teetered on the edge of a situation far worse than we'd come from.

I slipped my backup cell from my cleavage—yes, I knew now to always carry an extra—and called Mack first. It rang four times before he answered.

"Mack, it's Mia."

"Why the fuck haven't you been answering your phone?" he barked.

"King took it. He has me locked in a room in his house."

"Your house? Is the baby all right?"

"Arch is fine. I'm in a different house—a big old stone thing on a hill a few miles away."

"That used to be my place a few lifetimes ago."

"Well, I guess King kept it. I mean, one never knows when old things might become useful again. Hagne, for example? Seems he found a use for her, too."

"What the hell are you talking about?"

"She's back. In another body." *And I'm beyond crushed.* "I think he's with her, Mack. Her. Of all fucking people."

"So that's what he's doing. After I heard your message, I knew he got the chalice."

Oh, dear God. I felt like we were trapped in some horrible paranormal TV show. Only we weren't. That chalice was an ancient relic that was supposed to bring anyone back from the dead. King had used it to bring back Mack, who'd been stabbed by Teddi—a complete accident. Luckily, the chalice worked. Unluckily, Mack had died on sacred Native American soil and the souls who resided there wanted something in return for Mack. A trade. That was when King made his decision to swap his life for his brother's.

"I think he's bringing people back and putting them in 10 Club members' bodies," said Mack.

"Which people?" I asked.

"My best guess?"

"Yes," I replied.

"People who are dangerous and whom he can control."

Oh shit. If all the 10 Club members were loyal to King, then it would no longer be a free-for-all backstabbing competition. They'd all be rowing their depraved boats in the same direction and doing what he wanted. I simply couldn't imagine anyone having that much power. But what would he do with it?

"This is not good. Not good at all," I mumbled.

"Actually, this might help us," Mack said. "Anyone loyal to him will be loyal to me when I take over."

In theory that would be useful—he could more easily ambush people he controlled—however, not everyone used their eyes to determine a person's identity.

"You're assuming you can trick someone like Hagne." *Ugh. Fucking Hagne.* King had actually called her "my love" and kissed her hand. There was no bigger insult I could think of. It was the final knife in my broken heart.

"Don't worry; I can deal with her," Mack said. "But you need to get the hell out of there."

I was in so much shock, I'd almost forgotten I'd been locked in a room.

"Where are you now?" I asked.

"Since you flew off to Greece, I'm breaking into King's warehouse."

King's warehouse was booby-trapped up the yin-yang. "So you're about to die."

"Maybe. But so are you if you don't—"

"Ms. Turner, you never cease to amaze me," said King.

I spun on my heel. "Uh...gotta go." I dropped the phone from my ear, praying King had no idea that his brother and I had just been speaking or had a relationship. "I was just checking on...things at home."

"And I must remember to frisk you next time I lock you up." King's lips twisted into a sly smile.

"When so many monsters roam freely in the world, a girl should always take precautions." I batted my eyelashes.

"Are you referring to me or to Hagne?" he said, his voice low and velvety as he stepped in close, almost pressing his body to mine.

"Both." I glared up at him.

"Ah, yes. Hagne has told me about her run-in

with you," he said.

"She remembers?"

"Come with me. I would like to show you something." He turned, opened the door, and went into a room just across the hallway.

"How about just telling me what it is?" I called out. Surprises weren't my thing these days.

"Come, Ms. Turner!" he yelled.

I growled in protest, torn between running for it and seeing what he wanted to show me. *If he wanted me dead, I'd be dead by now.* And if I ran, he'd only catch me in two seconds—a perk of being a man without a real body.

"I do not have all night, Ms. Turner," King bellowed from the other room.

With hesitant steps, I followed the sound of his voice into his study. There was a desk, chair, crates of old books and a stack of scrolls piled to the side of the desk.

"Close the door behind you," he ordered.

"What is all this?" I said, doing as he asked.

King unrolled a long sheet of paper, his silvery eyes scanning the words. "I had Hagne write down every detail of my life—that which she is able to see with her gifts or remember."

"Is that why you brought her back?"

"Yes. I would like to understand why there are pieces missing from my memories."

"Why not just ask me instead of bringing back a psycho who once tried to kill you?"

He gave me a questioning look.

I shrugged. "You have her journals stored in your warehouse back in San Francisco. I read them once."

"Well, her gifts of sight are very powerful, and she is loyal to me now that I've given her back her life. She knows I can take it away at any time."

I wondered if that was why he hadn't used the chalice on himself. As a living man, he was limited to what he could do. That crawling around inside people's heads trick, for example? Nope. Killing someone with a snap of his fingers? Nope. He was much more dangerous in a non-corporeal state.

"So what have you learned from her?" I asked.

"Many interesting things." King's predatory eyes flickered with curiosity, and he stepped in closer. "But something she cannot explain is why I recall her but none of the moments involving you. So many lost memories." He ran his finger down my throat and began making small circles between my breasts. The sensation evoked strong memories of the two of us lying in bed, naked. The way he would drink me in with those eyes and study every inch of my body, as if committing each curve to memory. He always made me feel worshiped and desired.

He continued, "Hagne says you were everything to me." He leaned down and slid his lips across my cheek, and I couldn't lie; the heat of his skin and sound of his deep, sensual voice triggered flutters in my stomach and deep in my core. "So tell me, Mia, why would I leave behind memories of something so precious?"

My body shivered from his touch. It craved how good he could make me feel. "I don't know."

"Did you…" he placed a light kiss on my neck, "do something to anger me, perhaps?"

"No."

"You wouldn't be lying to me, now would you?" His lips went lower, over my collarbone, sparking goose bumps over my entire body.

I swallowed a sigh of longing. "No. I was loyal to you. I never would've hurt you like you hurt me." I stepped back, knowing he was pushing me dangerously close to something I didn't want to feel but hungered for. His body inside mine.

"Perhaps I found it easier to forget you than face you." He closed the gap between us and snaked his arm around my back.

I pulled my head away. "I guess we'll never know. But you have Hagne now."

"She is here to serve me, but not in that way. And now that she's told me who you really are, I am confident that you and I were meant to be together."

I tilted my head to the side. "Who do you think I really am?"

"The most powerful Seer ever to be born. One who has the gift to pass through the barriers of time, to see the dead, to see anything she wants."

"I don't know what Hagne told you, but I am

not a Seer anymore."

He shook his head slowly. "Hagne did not have to tell me anything. I assure you that the power still runs in your blood. How do you think I managed to resurrect five souls at once when the chalice usually allows for only one?"

"I really don't know," I said with a bite in my tone, "but if you were right, I'd go back to the moment you gave up the life we had."

"We can have it all back, Mia." He slid his hand to cup my cheek. His touch felt warm at first, but quickly turned hotter. Suddenly, I felt him pulsing inside me, through my veins. This time it didn't hurt. It felt sensual and intimate, like he was rubbing up against my soul and embracing me.

I wanted to pull away but couldn't. I missed this too much—that connection and closeness. He was the love of my life, and as much as I wanted to tell myself that this was not the same man, the lie was what I craved. I needed to feel him close one more time. I needed to feel his breath on my neck and hear his soft, deep groans in my ears. I needed to feel his lips and cock and hands touching me everywhere. I needed to fill that hole in my heart and breathe again even if it only lasted a moment.

"This is what you want, isn't it?" Lust twinkled in his gray eyes. He pulled me in tighter, allowing me to feel his erection. "There, you see. I haven't forgotten you completely. And with time, I might remember everything. Don't you want that?"

Dammit. He had found that thread of hope inside me and knew just how to tug.

He continued, "Perhaps this is fate playing out as it is meant to be."

I stared up at him, wanting some sign of truth, but all I saw was need. His and mine.

He leaned down and kissed me. His silky lips felt warm and sensual, exactly like I remembered. This was still King. Still seductive and carnal. Still able to evoke primal lust deep inside me.

I gave in, fully aware of what I was about to do: Make a mistake.

He pushed me back onto the desk and lifted my ass on top of it. His hands, strong and warm, slid behind my knees and parted them. His fingers began to roam, touching the delicate skin inside my thigh.

I let out a soft moan, sinking into the moment.

His mouth broke away from my lips and trailed heated kisses down the side of my neck, his thick stubble tickling the delicate skin.

"Tell me, Mia," he said in a slow deep voice, "is this the way we always feel together?"

One hand brushed over the apex between my legs, sending a sharp sexual ache pulsing through my core, while his other hand moved to my breast, cupping it over the navy blue fabric.

"Yes," I whispered.

He slid his hand down the front of my panties and delved his finger between my heated folds.

"You're already wet for me."

King only had to look at me a certain way, and I would be ready.

My body jolted involuntarily as he slid a thick finger inside, testing me. "Tell me how it felt, Mia, when we made her, when I put that baby inside you."

I panted lightly, enjoying the sensation of his finger pumping. "It was early in the morning, and I found you in your study."

"A study like this one?"

"Yes." I panted.

His mouth returned to mine, kissing me hard. "And what next?"

"You put me on top of your desk, like you're doing now."

His hand moved faster, stoking the fire, pushing me closer.

"And then?" He unzipped himself, freeing his cock.

"And then you slid inside me," I whispered.

He removed his hand, pushed my black lace thong aside, and placed the head of his shaft at my entrance. "Like this?" He thrust into me.

I gasped and closed my eyes, feeling my body melt into him and him into me. He was like a sexual drug my body had been craving.

"Yes," I replied.

King pumped his hips slowly, taking the time to grind at the end of each thrust, triggering a gasp each time. "Like this, Mia. Is this how you like to get fucked?"

"Yes." He was so good at it.

He withdrew his cock, pushed me down on the desk, and slid off my panties. He undid his pants the rest of the way, allowing me to see him—his hard thick cock, the dark hair around its base, the heavy balls hanging between his legs.

He pulled my body closer to him, bringing my entrance just to the edge of the desk. "I want you to watch me fucking you, Mia. I want you to remember this as our first fuck. The old King is gone. Do you understand?" He pushed himself into me, driving hard, taking not giving.

My body reacted with a sensual contraction. "No."

He hit me again with another thrust. "He is gone, Mia. You have me now." He slammed his cock into me, so rough, so delicious. I thought he was going to continue insisting I forget the man who truly owned my heart, but perhaps he'd gone too far, needing release more than my submission.

He leaned over me, claiming me with his lips, his body hammering forcefully. His hand slid behind my knee to deepen his penetration. His other hand scooped behind my back to hold me in place.

My body opened to him, my legs parted wide, needing to feel him as deep as he could go, while my heart stayed closed. I knew in the back of my mind that this wasn't King. Not the whole man—the one with a bit of darkness inside his tough, but loving heart. This man could never be trusted. Still, I needed him. Just one more time.

King withdrew his mouth and pushed his forehead to mine, stilling his hips with his cock wedged deep inside me. His masculine, guttural groan told me he was coming. I loved it when he came—the thought of my body pleasing the man I loved, the moment he poured his cum into me, the sound of his breath and deep voice intermingling in my ears. I loved how he never got enough of my lips and breasts and how he made me come over and over again with his thick shaft.

The carnal explosion deep in my belly ignited and paralyzed my entire body, sending my mind into a delicious fog of pleasure. King pulsed his hips, watching with hooded eyes as he milked the waves of my climax.

"That's right, Mia. Come for me, like you did for him."

Never. But in my mind we were there in our study at home on that morning he gave me our daughter. It was a moment when my body connected to him in a way it hadn't before, so filled with love. Then I felt a spark somewhere deep inside my belly. With Archon, I remember feeling something calm and bright tingling inside me, but that came weeks later. With her, it was instant. And now I knew why.

She is a Seer. A powerful one. Perhaps it had been her blood King sensed.

As for me, feeling King lying over me, inside my body, all I felt was sadness. The afterglow, the full feeling of our bodies joined, had been lacking. An empty fuck riding on memories of love.

King kissed my lips, slow and sensual, and then withdrew. He immediately went to putting himself away, avoiding eye contact.

Strange. I sat up, slid off the desk, and began arranging my dress. My eyes quickly searched for my black thong, and I noticed King sliding something into his pocket.

My panties.

Okay. He wanted to keep them but wouldn't look at me?

An awkward silence filled the room. My silence was more of a state of mourning, but I couldn't begin to guess what was going on inside his head.

King straightened his tie and reached for the door. "Be in the basement in five minutes." He disappeared and left the door wide open while I stood there staring at the empty space. *What the hell was that?* He'd seemed genuinely troubled or disturbed or something after fucking me.

Had he remembered something?

"Well, well, well, looks like the old king still has a thing for you."

I looked up to find Hagne standing in the hallway just past the door in her garish red dress.

Funny, I could almost recognize her from the glint of hatred in her blue eyes, even though when I'd met her, she'd been a brown beauty—dark eyes, dark hair, dark skin. But there was no mistaking that glare. All Hagne.

I lifted my chin and walked past her. "And it looks like the old king still thinks of you as his little bitch."

CHAPTER NINE

After I left the study, I slipped into the bathroom, fixed myself up and thought about my next move. I had to assume that I had gotten through to King somehow and that being physical had been the key.

This was good.

King wanting me like that, wanting to hear about making our daughter, meant the emotional connection wasn't gone or that he craved it on some level. What bothered me, however, was his complete lack of warmth. No, I didn't mean physically. King was his old hot self. But his soul felt icier than ever.

It's like that part of him is all broken. Or maybe gone altogether? I patted my face with a tissue, reset my straightened curls with a quick finger comb, and made my way outside. I had a few days, if that, to determine what had happened to King after he died and what he really planned to do with these resurrected demons from his past.

I entered the cozy living room—cozy by King's standards since it wouldn't hold a hundred people—and instantly realized that many of the formally dressed guests were the same people from San Francisco. There were many faces I didn't recognize, too.

And no Hagne. *Thank God.*

I walked over by the stone fireplace and pretended to admire the painting above it while I stole glances of the guests and committed their faces to memory. The painting, by the way? Scary as fuck. Some old demon eating a heart it had just ripped out of a naked man.

Someone clanked a wineglass at the far end of the room, grabbing everyone's attention.

King. He stood there looking handsome as hell in his tux, flashing a cocky smile. He'd gotten over whatever had bothered him after our little encounter in his study.

"My esteemed guests," he called out across the room of elegantly dressed people, "as you know, I've invited you all here tonight to usher in a new dawn of 10 Club. You are the elite of our group, the powerful, the people with vision who understand what 10 Club will become once we cease operating under a veil of secrecy. Today we live in the shadows. Tomorrow we live and breathe and bathe in the light, molding the world into a new shape, where the weak gladly accept their places and where the powerful few rule them." King raised his glass to the guests, who applauded with enthusiasm. "As it was meant to be!"

I stood there with my mouth hanging open. I

mean, the world had seen its fair share of dark times, but this? This would be nothing in comparison if 10 Club came out of the evil closet.

"Oh, I can't wait to find out what powers he gives me," said the woman to my side.

The man next to her, one I thought I recognized from San Francisco, replied, "I hear that King is giving out something very special tonight. Perhaps mind-reading abilities."

So…these people, whom I'll call the newbies, believed they were getting free gifts?

I wanted to tsk at them. *Nothing in this world is free, you idiots.*

The applause died down and King continued, "And now, my dear people, if the ten guests of honor will follow me?"

The room applauded again as three women and seven men stepped forward.

Ten? He's doing ten at a time now? And from the conversation I'd just overheard, I didn't think any of them had a clue that they were about to be evicted from their bodies.

This is bad. Not that I felt sorry for these animals parading around as human beings in formal wear, but the souls taking their places would be much worse.

"Ms. Turner," King called out, giving me a stern warning with his eyes not to mess this up, "your presence is required."

Oh, God. I did not want to help him, but what

choice did I have? I couldn't run, he'd kill me if I said no, and I needed to be in a position to help Mack or save King. *Or both.*

I took a steady breath and followed the herd through the formal dining room with an enormous crystal chandelier and through a small hallway to a door where King revealed a flight of narrow dark stairs.

Standing at the end of the conga line behind a woman in a sequined white gown, I groaned. I knew what would happen down there. King would perform his bloody ritual and bring ten people back from the grave.

As I descended the wooden stairs, the sound of everyone's heels filling the narrow dark passage with thumping sounds, I had to wonder if King could bring all of these people back, why couldn't I resurrect him a second time? I mean, I could guess why he wouldn't want that—he was much more powerful in his nonliving state. But what if I forced him somehow? Would he become whole again, or would he simply be the same dark soul in a body?

It was worth a try.

I entered the dark basement and stood in the corner. This time, I watched King's every move, listened to every word, and memorized every symbol he painted on the walls and floor before he called me forward.

"Let me do it," I said, taking his knife. If I had to bleed, I wanted to control the knife.

King's gaze turned carnal and hungry as I cut my palm and collected the blood for him.

I think I just earned his trust.

After the blood ceremony, the ten people who left the basement were not the same ten souls who'd entered. I'd been right; the dinner party before—the speech, formality, and introductions—had all been a sham. Because after the ceremony, I watched as old friends embraced, laughed, toasted and screamed with delight in strange languages. It felt like an international reunion for old college buddies. Then I spotted Hagne greeting a brunette woman who had tears in her eyes. I could practically feel the energy spiking in that corner of the room where they stood. Even the little life in my belly began to flutter around, almost as if in a panic.

Oh crap.

My eyes searched the room for King, who had disappeared after the ceremony. I planned to get him alone again if I could. I wanted to find out when the next shindig was scheduled. Then I'd call Mack and propose a plan. We'd hijack the ceremony and bring back King.

I took a sip of my ginger ale, trying to settle my stomach. *Calm down, little Ariadna.* That was what I planned to name my daughter. It meant daughter of a king.

"Ms. Turner?"

I swiveled and found King all cleaned up, a fresh new tux, glowering down at me with those steely gray eyes.

"Yes?"

"Would you come with me?"

I wanted to, but I didn't like his aggressive tone. Especially since there was no reason for it.

"Why?" I asked.

"*Come* with me," he repeated sternly.

"Are you going to hurt us?" Yes, I said "us." I wasn't going to dance around the truth with him.

"No." He grabbed my arm and tugged.

"Wait. Is anyone else going to hurt us?"

His eyes flickered with annoyance. "No." He turned and headed from the room.

I followed along, feeling my back stiffen as he led me away from the party to a small sitting room with a cozy fire just off the entryway.

He turned and looked down at me.

"What?" I said.

His mouth lunged for mine and his arms embraced me possessively. My body froze for a moment, wondering what was happening. But then I noticed something: His passion.

What is going on?

His hand moved to cup my cheek, and his kiss deepened.

So much emotion poured from him that I felt instantly dizzy. *He's coming around. He has to be.* I melted into him and let his tongue dance with mine. I should've known that all he needed was a taste of our love. King's heart couldn't forget me. That had to be why he'd behaved so strangely after we had sex.

King snapped back with a wild look in his eyes. "You are fucking amazing, Mia. Together we'll be unstoppable." He slid his hand over my stomach.

Whoa. Wait. "Do you remember me at all, King?"

"I told you, Mia, that man you married, he is gone. He will never return. But what you and I can have will be so much better. No one will ever threaten you again. No one will touch you. You will have the world at your feet and the life of the queen you were meant to be."

A queen? Is that what he thought I wanted?

In my gut, I knew this was a pivotal moment. A moment when I threw in the kitchen sink—my faith, my hope, my love—and prayed things would work out, that I would get through to him eventually and get him back. Or I threw in the towel, lied through my teeth, and manipulated him, knowing that he told the truth: It was over for us. The man I loved was really gone, and the best I could hope for was to end this dark version of him and the 10 Club.

My heart sank into a deep, dark hole. This moment felt like losing him all over again. Because, goddammit, history had taught me that hoping didn't do a damned thing. If I wanted to live and wanted my children to be free of all this, I had to put them first. I didn't have the luxury of simply waiting to see what might happen.

I filled my mind with pleasant memories of yesterday so that King would sense the joy inside me. I remembered the day we married on the beach not too far from our home here in Crete. I remembered how he made love to me, held me, and begged me to swear I would never leave his side because he loved me so much. I thought about the look in his eyes when he held Arch in his arms for the first time and realized that his pain and suffering for thousands of years was all worth it because he'd been given a second chance to live and to be a father.

I gazed at the reflection of the flames from the fireplace dancing in King's silvery eyes. "I don't know, King. I mean, who are these people? Can they really be trusted not to hurt us?" I asked, knowing I had to put up a little fight, or he wouldn't buy my act. I needed him to trust me.

"You have nothing to fear," he said. "As long as you vow to forget the old King and be loyal to me." He leaned down, placing us nose to nose.

Oh shit. The flames in his eyes were not from the fireplace. "What happened to you?" I whispered.

"Progress. And you cannot stop it, Mia. No one can."

The hairs on the back of my neck stood up.

King pinched my chin, pinning me with those

demonic-looking eyes. "I can see you want to hold on to the past, Mia. But you must let go. Your husband is a memory."

I couldn't make sense of this. "What happened to you?" I repeated.

Exasperated, he shook his head. "Who the hell cares?"

"I do."

He chuckled sadistically. "Do you know who that man really was, Mia? Do you know what you're hanging on to?"

"Of course I do."

"No. You do not. I've learned quite a lot about this man you seem to worship so much—this man I once was." He shook his head. "So weak. So soft."

I felt a spark of anger. "He was a good person."

King frowned. "Really?" Our bodies close, he leaned down to whisper in my ear, "Did you know he fucked Talia the day before he died?"

What? Talia had been King's partner in crime for many years. From what he told me, things fell apart when she decided she wanted more from him and he refused. Then his life became tangled with mine and he cut her out completely. She had not been happy about that.

I stepped back. "What are you talking about?"

An evil joy twinkled in his eyes. "It's true. This man that you would throw away your life for, that you hold up on a pedestal, he was unfaithful to you. He fucked that woman in a hotel room in Vegas."

"I don't believe you. He would never." He hated Talia. She was like an evil cockroach he wanted to crush.

"It's true," I heard a curvy brunette say from the foyer. She was one of the women from the circle who'd just been talking to Hagne. "He fucked me to get his hands on that chalice. Once I told him where it was, he killed me." She laughed.

"Talia?" I muttered.

She sauntered over with a familiar wiggle in her hips. "Back from the dead, you little bitch."

I had no clue she'd died; however, I felt so cold inside that I didn't have the strength to get angry or feel anything other than my heart shredding into sad little ribbons.

Talia continued, standing to King's side. "That's right. He fucked me up against the wall like an angry beast. I told him sooner or later I'd have something he'd want and get what I wanted." She sighed contentedly. "It was so worth getting strangled for."

Wait. This just doesn't make sense. King would never. "You're both making it up."

King shook his head. "My, my, Mia. You are a stubborn one. Just as everyone says. But why don't you ask my brother's woman, Teddi. She was there."

My head spun, and my heart felt nonexistent as everything suddenly went from bad to worse. *So King cheated on me. He fucking cheated on me? For*

Mack? Fucking Mack? My heart couldn't make sense of all this. King chose his brother over his children and wife. And he fucking cheated on me?

"Oh no. Is the little Seer cunt feeling hurt?" the new Talia mock pouted.

The rage clicked on inside me, and I exploded. "You evil fucking bitch!" I lunged for her, and she fell to the floor.

I put my hands around her neck and squeezed. Her face twisted as she tried to push me off, but couldn't. "You disgusting piece of shit." I tightened with both hands, watching her face turn red.

"All right, Ms. Turner," King said with a chuckle, threading his arms under mine and pulling me up. "Let the mean lady go. I didn't bring her back from the dead so you could kill her all over again."

I hung on to Talia's neck as long as I could, but King pried my fingers loose.

Once free, Talia gasped and stumbled to her feet, rubbing her neck. "I'll fucking kill you," she croaked. "You and your little baby. I'll skin him alive and make you watch."

If there was one thing I'd learned about 10 Club members, it was that they never made idle threats and they never let go of grudges.

"Not if I kill you first!" I spat. Blinded by anger, my eyes quickly swept the room. I grabbed a wrought-iron table lamp and swung. It landed right on her temple with a loud crack and Talia dropped to the floor. "You think you fucking scare me?" I yelled at her immobile body. I raised the lamp to finish her. No one threatened my baby. No one.

"That is enough, Ms. Turner," King roared and snatched the lamp from my hand.

I pointed my finger in his face, screaming, "You fuck her? You break your vows to me with this disgusting bitch? You leave *everything* behind that was good in your life for this? For fucking *this*?" I pushed him, but it did nothing. He wasn't a real man. He was made of illusions and powers, but not real skin and bones.

"This," he replied with a calm but fierce tone, "is the only thing that matters. Power. And now you see what not having it will do to people—they must compromise, beg, and steal to get what they want. They are at the mercy of others." He grabbed my still-sore wrist. "If your pathetic husband had had more power, he surely wouldn't have had to fuck her to help his brother."

"You want to see power?" I snapped my arm away and stuck my middle finger in his face. "Fuck you, King. You and the 10 Club."

I turned and left the room, knowing full well I wasn't alone. He was right there with me. I could smell him in the air, feel him on my skin, but I wouldn't give him the satisfaction of saying anything.

I walked past several guests, who glided into the party, looking joyous and elegant. All 10 Club members, I assumed, who were about to be sold a giant pile of festering bullcrap and then later used as vessels for King's little army. Or big army. I didn't know how far he would go and how many people he would bring back. All I knew was that King was rounding up some of the most vile, cruel, sadistic people ever to walk this earth. Even people who'd once been his enemies. He probably enjoyed making them bow down to him and lick his boots.

Sadistic prick.

I made my way down the edge of the driveway, walking beside a never-ending line of expensive cars and chauffeurs congregating in small groups, smoking cigarettes, and chatting about whatever 10 Club help talked about.

About fifteen cars down, I spotted Arno frowning at me as I approached. I suddenly slammed into a wall and nearly fell back.

I blinked, but there was nothing there. Nothing I could see.

Fucking King.

"Get the hell out of my way," I snapped.

"Have dinner with me tomorrow night."

"Screw you." I tried to step around him but only ended up hitting that wall again. I must've looked like a crazy drunk to anyone watching.

"What if I want to make you a proposal? One you'll want to hear," he said.

King and his stupid deals. "Another one? What about the one where you promise never to act like an ancient douche bag, cheating, selfish tyrant and then break that promise? No, thank you."

"No. This one is for your brother."

My body froze, and my heart tightened in my chest.

"You've now seen I have the power to bring anyone back as long as I have a body to give them."

In my mind, there was no excuse for what King had done or how he'd hurt me, but I couldn't deny that Justin's death, the impact it had on me and my parents, had been devastating. Justin had been a good person with an enormous heart, whose only mistake was getting involved with Vaughn, 10 Club's president at the time. Vaughn, a sick psychopath, somehow ended up being the financial backer for Justin's big archeological dig in Southern Mexico. In exchange, Vaughn would get dibs on anything of interest Justin unearthed. It all ended badly, of course. Justin somehow got involved with Vaughn's mistress—Vaughn's property under 10 Club law—and then Justin tried to free her after he found something important at the dig site. He thought he could use it as a bargaining chip of sorts. Justin didn't stand a chance. The mistress, pregnant mistress, didn't either.

I killed Vaughn for what he did to Justin and the woman carrying his baby, but it hadn't erased the pain. The only peace it gave me was knowing that Vaughn could no longer go after my mother and father, who he'd promised to skin alive on camera and have sex with. *Sick, sick fucker.*

"Not interested," I lied, knowing King would leverage this to its fullest if I showed too much interest. Once again, I tried to move past the invisible force blocking my way.

"Sir, back away from Mrs. Minos." Arno stood at my side, snarling like a rabid pit bull, his eyes locked right onto something next to me.

"Arno, old friend. So nice to see you." King did not show himself.

"We are *not* friends. Step away from her."

"Or what?" King asked.

"Or the Spiros will keep their vow," Arno said calmly.

"Dinner at the Kapsalian," said King. "Nine o'clock." And just like that, King was gone, the air around us cool and still.

"Let's go." Arno held out his elbow, gesturing for me to take it. My knees jittering and my heart in a state of toxic meltdown, I latched on and allowed him to help me into the back of the limo.

Arno quickly had us heading home.

"The vow you mentioned, what was that about?" I asked.

Arno remained silent.

"Okay. You can't tell me what it is, but this has to be something recent. I mean, otherwise, I would've heard all about it."

Arno made a subtle nod.

"Was this vow made before King left to go help Mack?"

Arno nodded.

Dammit. Another confirmation that King had known what might happen. He'd planned contingencies.

"Is it the kind of thing King would make you do if I were in trouble?" I asked.

Arno remained silent.

"Okay. He made you swear not to tell me or anyone. But King knew something bad was going to happen, didn't he?"

"He believed it was a possibility."

Fuck. And that meant he'd taken precautions for us. Just like he had with the wards around the property. He'd also made the Spiros loyal to me.

"Arno, if King were about to hurt me, would this vow become relevant?"

"You know I cannot say anything, Mrs. Minos. Not without risking my family's well-being."

Of course I wouldn't want that. But whatever King had told them could be used to hurt him and protect us.

"Is it lot number ninety-four?" I asked, taking a stab.

Arno's dark eyes shot me a very stern look.

That has to be it. Something in that warehouse they could use if things turned out for the worst.

"Just tell me, do you know what's in lot ninety-four?" I asked.

"I do not."

"But you know how to get to it," I said.

He gave me a look indicating he might. "Please. I cannot say anything, Mrs. Minos. Simply know that precautions were made. Your husband was not a stupid man."

I leaned back in the seat. So whatever was in that warehouse could kill King if things went south. And King had told Arno how to get at it, but not what it was or likely how to use it. Mack knew what it was—clearly. He'd been trying to break into that warehouse to get it.

So King gave two people he trusted, more or less, everything they needed to end him. But why not me? Why wouldn't he tell me?

Because he cheated on me. And King was afraid to put his life in my hands.

I laughed bitterly. *Oh, King, how well you know me.*

CHAPTER TEN

I'm not going to lie; King had me by the balls. I had to show up for dinner and listen to his proposal. But what would he want from me in exchange for Justin's life? I knew King wanted my cooperation, my blood, and my loyalty. Was there something else? I didn't know, but I had to remember that I wasn't without my own bargaining chips.

So against Arno's advice, I decided to go tonight. Mack had been MIA since our conversation yesterday evening at King's place, which made me wonder if something terrible had happened to him in that warehouse. Honestly, Mack wasn't a weakling or naïve. He knew exactly what traps and dangers awaited anyone who tried to break in. Hell, he'd worked for King for…well, I didn't know exactly how long, but a few centuries at the very least.

So after a few failed attempts at reaching Mack, I ended up calling Teddi, but she didn't answer. I wasn't sure what I'd say anyway. "Hi, it's Mia. Is Mack okay? Great. Now fuck you! Why didn't you tell me that King screwed around on me for that damned chalice? Huh? Huh?" Make no mistake, I'd saved Teddi's ass one or two times when things with Mack were not in a good place and King saw her as a threat to Mack. It hurt that she would keep something like this from me.

You can't trust anyone, Mia. When will you learn that? I had to accept that I was alone in this world now and it was up to me to look after Arch and Ariadna. No one else.

I put on a black sweater, jeans, and black leather boots. I knew King would prefer something sexy and feminine, but I wasn't going there to have breakup sex or get him to look at me. We were done. Done. Done. I just wanted to hear the terms of his deal.

Just after nine o'clock, Arno pulled up to the Kapsalian, which was a historic hotel tucked into a lush green hillside bursting with olive trees and magnificent views of the valley below. I hadn't explored Crete all that much since agreeing to live here as our home base, but that was only because we'd taken the first six months of marriage to go on a honeymoon on King's yacht. When Arch was born, I had him in San Francisco and stayed at my parents' home for four weeks before coming to King's home. We'd only been there for a short time before things with Mack began to unravel and we had to come back to the US looking for him.

I slid from the car and asked Arno to stay close.

This wouldn't take long.

I made my way down the walkway toward the hotel's restaurant. The entire estate looked lovely, built of stone with arched doorways and white plaster. It was about as elegant and rustic as you could get in Crete without jumping into the category of Ancient Greece's massive temples built in honor of the gods.

I approached the restaurant's arched doorway covered in twinkling white lights, where a young woman in black heels asked for my name. I gave it and she showed me through the surprisingly empty restaurant, out to a terrace with a view of the town below. I suspected that King rented out the place for the night. That was his move. And it no longer impressed me.

"Ms. Turner." Dressed in a finely tailored black suit, King's tall, imposing frame rose from the table, and he came around to slide out my chair.

I walked out alone, determined to make this quick. "You can drop the chivalry. I'm here for business. Nothing more."

"I like a woman who knows how to cut to the chase." He waited for me to be seated anyway.

I sat begrudgingly. "You like a woman who grovels and cowers as she licks the heels of your polished shoes."

"You are mistaken." He took his seat across from me and leaned those broad shoulders back. "I can't stand submissive women."

"Oh. That's right. I almost forgot. You like it when they fight. It makes the fun of crushing their souls so much more enjoyable."

He laughed. "You know me so well."

The waitress walked up, and he ordered me a scotch, neat, and himself a martini.

"No, thanks. I'll have mineral water," I corrected.

King looked down at my stomach as the young woman scurried off with a nervous-looking posture.

"My apologies." He dipped his head. "I almost forgot. And I thank you for taking such care with my daughter."

My fists balled under the table. "She's not really yours, now is she?"

"Of course she is."

"Funny, when it comes to talking about the things you did before your last encounter with death—cheating, for example, or promises you made to people—you wash your hands. But you will take credit for my baby?"

"What can I say? I'm a man. I take responsibility when it conveniences me." He flashed that trademark smile across the table.

"All right, King. I don't have time for your games. Name your price." I folded my arms and sat back in the chair.

"Oh," he leaned in, "but Ms. Turner, I was about to tell you how much I enjoyed our fuck yesterday—the taste of your lips, the creamy heat between your thighs, the way you moaned when I came inside you."

I lifted my brows, hoping he'd see the middle fingers sticking out of them. I had loved this man. More than my own life. Now he treated my heart like a game?

"Eh…yeah, no. There is nothing you can say to me, King, that will get me where you want to go. Not to your bed, your desk, your side—nowhere. So I'll give you ten seconds to tell me what you want in exchange for Justin and then I'm getting up from this table."

His devilish smile melted away. "You push hard for a woman who holds no cards."

"I hold plenty and telling you what they are is a rooky move. Speak. Five seconds."

King tilted his head and stared.

"Okay." I stood. "Have a nice life, if that's what you call your evil existence."

"Vaughn or Justin, Ms. Turner. Which would you like me to bring back? Because the choice is all yours."

I stopped in my tracks. *Fuck. Fuck! Fuck!* I had not seen that coming.

I slowly sat back down, trying to keep my breathing steady despite the sheer terror now clawing at my insides. How the hell did this man always know the way to motivate me? *The asshole doesn't even remember me.*

Oh, but he's been calling out the dead, who know

plenty.

"I'm listening, King. But if you bring back Vaughn, he'll kill me. Me and this baby." Along with everyone in my family after he skinned them alive.

"Oh, Ms. Turner," he placed his elbows on the table, a happy evil gleam in his beautiful silvery eyes, "what makes you think I would allow that?"

The waitress showed up with our drinks and quickly fled the scene. She must've sensed the malevolence buzzing around in the cool night air.

King lifted his frosty-looking martini, sipped appreciatively, and set the delicate glass on the white tablecloth. "I would make him wait to kill you after the baby was born. Do you think me a barbarian?"

"Wow. You are…" I lacked the words, so I went with a very sarcastic, "awesome."

"I am a man who gets what he wants."

"And what do you want? Oh, wait." I stuck out my palm. "I want you, Ms. Turner," I said in a deep mocking voice.

He snickered arrogantly. "Very good, Mia."

Not really. King was very predictable when it came to me. "So I agree to be yours and you'll give me back Justin."

"I think the more accurate way to summarize the situation is that you agree to be mine, and I won't bring back Vaughn. Oh, yes. And you get to live and be a mother to your children."

He had to have thought this through. Meaning,

he knew he might be able to back me into a corner with his threats, but sooner or later, I'd try to find a way to change the game. That meant he would use whatever leverage he could to keep me in check in perpetuity, and there was only one thing—make that two—he could ever really use against me.

No. No. I am not allowing this shit to happen. I would not say yes to a lifetime of being his doormat while he did what he wanted to me and used my children as leverage.

I rose from the table, holding back the urge to spit in his gorgeous face. "No fucking deal. I won't become your little toy and let you use our babies to keep me in check. I won't live my life with someone whose word is worthless and whose heart is a bottomless dark pit. And as for Vaughn," I planted my hands on the table, snarling, "bring it the fuck on. I killed him once. I am *not* afraid to kill him again. And if you come near me, King, if you threaten me, it will be your downfall. Ironically, you made sure of that." He had to know that Arno and Mack held the key to ending him by his own design. I laughed. "You fucked yourself."

In an instant, King had me dangling in his powerful hand by the neck. "Watch yourself, Ms. Turner. That baby won't be inside you forever." He set me down, and I clutched my neck.

"You can't break me, King, because I'm done being afraid." I straightened my back, stood up on my tiptoes, and pulled his mouth down to mine. I kissed him hard and then let him go. "No one loved you as much as I did, King. No one. And that's the funny thing about love; it can turn so easily into hate."

He nodded with a laugh. "Dear god, Ms. Turner, you are so delightful. I am going to enjoy breaking you immensely."

Just like that, King was gone. I drew an exasperated breath and looked up at the starry night, praying for strength and patience. My lack of submission had just made him more determined than ever to break me. He would never stop. He would never let go.

A bitter chill swept through my body. I knew now what had to be done. I had to get my hands on lot ninety-four and pull the proverbial trigger.

I slid into the awaiting limo. "Drive, Arno."

"Everything alright, ma'am?"

"No. But it will be."

Thirty minutes later, we pulled up to the house and found a red Ferrari parked in the driveway. *Mack!* Only he would rent a freaking Ferrari from the airport. He loved cars. And planes and guns and all that tough-guy shit.

I walked in the front door and found Mack standing there waiting for me.

"So when do we kill King?" I asked.

CHAPTER ELEVEN

Mack and I sat in the living room with its panoramic view of the ocean that was now just a sea of darkness. *So fitting. That's how I feel inside.*

I quickly placed my hand on my stomach, correcting myself. The little Seer inside me could not be allowed to grow with so much hate and anger. I had to focus on the light at the end of the tunnel, which for me was knowing my babies would be safe.

"I'm sorry for not telling you about Talia." Mack rose from the couch across from me and began pacing the length of the open room with bright white furniture—King's favorite. "Teddi is sorry, too. But we didn't see the point. King was dead, and we already knew how hard it was for you to accept that he traded his life for mine."

I nodded, grinding my jaw, arms crossed, staring out into the abyss.

He continued, "I'm sorry, Mia. But we only wanted to protect you and let you focus on Arch and putting your life back together…and…" He blew out a breath. "This hasn't been easy for any of us. You have to know that."

He and Teddi didn't understand that they were a part of my life, too. And then to find out they'd been hiding things from me? That I couldn't fully trust them? It was goddamned painful. They'd saved me from nothing.

"Fine. What's done is done," I said, knowing we had bigger fish to fry. "Where's Teddi now?"

"Theodora is here on the island with me. She's at the hotel, resting right now."

Teddi was Theodora's nickname and it didn't fit her one bit. She was a Seer who would become extremely powerful once she learned how to control her gifts. At least, that was my assumption. But the name Teddi sounded warm and fuzzy and harmless.

"I guess that's why you guys weren't answering your phones," I said, thinking out loud. They'd both been on a plane. "But I'm surprised you brought her with you."

"I feel better when she's with me. She's pregnant, Mia." Mack's voice was filled with heaviness.

I turned to look at him. "That's great news." They weren't married yet, but they both wanted kids. Didn't really matter the order.

"No, it's fucking scary as hell news. This is a bad time." Mack ran his hands through his dark hair, and it pained me to look at him. He and King truly were identical.

"I'm pregnant, too," I said. "So I fully comprehend where you're coming from."

Mack's blue, blue eyes widened with shock. "Wow. Congratulations?"

I nodded solemnly. We all knew that these were dangerous times. "Thanks."

"Well, that just makes this all the more important for us to finish."

"Did you get lot ninety-four?" I asked.

"Yes. Arno called yesterday and told me how to get it."

I shot up from the couch. "He did?"

"He said that King had threatened your life, and it was time since the criteria King gave him had been met."

Why hadn't Arno said anything? Of course, he was a man of few words.

"What was the criteria?" I asked.

"King apparently left us both notes. They said that if things went wrong and he came back again, that we were to use lot ninety-four to protect you and Arch if he wasn't…in control."

We all knew what that looked like. Before I'd brought King back, he'd had different points in his life where the curse inside him made him do horrible things. He'd killed, tortured, and even punished himself. Eventually, he'd learned tricks and acquired strange tattoos that helped him keep the demons at bay.

"Okay. So this is good," I said, not actually meaning it. Nothing about this was good.

Mack took a glass vial from his pocket and

placed it on the glass coffee table next to the couch where I sat.

"What's that?"

"Lot ninety-four. It's a vial of ink."

Ink? I cocked a brow.

He reached into his other pocket and pulled out a folded piece of paper.

"What are you planning to do?" I asked. "Write King a note that says please die?"

"This is the blood of Kalamos, the Greek god of the reed, or pen, if you will. You write the names of your enemies on paper and they will die."

I laughed. *How stupid.* "Great. We're totally fucked."

"Do you think King would leave behind a joke to protect your life?"

"No. But the blood of a god?"

"That's what it's called. That doesn't mean it's really the blood of a god. Our people in ancient times were big fans of giving things dramatic names."

"Then what is it?" I asked.

"Ink. Very powerful and deadly ink."

I wrapped my head around it reluctantly. "So it's a death curse of sorts."

"Yes."

"And where does its power come from?" Objects with power didn't pop up in gardens. They had to be made and given power by people who had it.

"My guess? It came from Seer blood."

I rubbed my face. King had killed a lot of Seers. His hate for them had been deeply seeded in his hate for Hagne and her family, who were the reason his people died. He'd wanted to rid the world of their kind in retaliation. Of course, I was a Seer, too, but he never saw me as the enemy. *Well, that's all changing.*

"Okay. So what do we do?" I expected we'd have to do some elaborate spell.

"We write his name on the paper."

"That's it?" Seemed too easy.

"That's it."

"And King won't be able to come back this time?"

"This curse doesn't merely kill the body, it kills the soul. They cannot come back because there is nothing left."

My blood curdled in my veins. This was it. The moment we ended King. And with him, any hope of ever getting back what I'd lost, even if that hope was the size of a speck of dust, would die. I would have to mourn him all over again.

I drew a breath. "I will do it." I felt I owed King and our memory that much.

"We can't."

I blinked away my forming tears. "Why not?"

"We need the names of the 10 Club members first."

My brain connected the dots. "King is the only one who knows who all of the members are." And I didn't just mean the names on their birth certificates or passports. Some of these people were not who they appeared to be on the outside.

"Yes. So if we only kill King, 10 Club will—"

"Keep going," I surmised. "Another person will step up and take over. They've all got to die." I shook my head. *Fuck. Why does this just keep getting harder?* "King is not going to give us those names."

"He will if he has to choose between them or himself."

"So you want to threaten him, get the names, and then stab him in the back and put his name on the list anyway."

"Yes."

"What's your plan to keep King from just lopping your head off before you have a chance to do anything?"

"You and Theodora are staying here in the compound, where it's safe. I'll be on the phone with you so you can write down names as we go. King can't get in here." Mack unfolded the piece of paper, pulled out an old nib pen, and uncorked the bottle. He dipped the tip into the dark red liquid and began writing. I watched as he spelled out the letters K, I, and N. He then handed it to me. "If anything happens, anything at all, you put down a G, Mia. Are we clear?"

"And then what?"

"I go to plan B."

"You're going to take over 10 Club."

"Yes. I'll step in as King and gather names from the inside. It will simply take longer and present more of a risk."

I walked over to the window and looked out across the dark ocean, feeling the weight of the world on my shoulders. "I hate your plan. I hate everything about it and this situation."

"You think I want to kill King? He's been half of my soul for three thousand years and there isn't anything I wouldn't do for him. But I know that this wasn't what he wanted for us. I know he would want me to kill him if it came to this, and I didn't need a note from him to tell me that. But make no mistake, when he dies, a piece of me will die with him, and I won't ever get it back or feel whole again without him."

I looked down at my trembling hands. "When are you going to see him?"

"Tonight. Theodora's just waiting for me to tell her to come here." He shrugged. "I wanted to talk things out with you first."

He slid out his phone and dialed. "Hey, it's me. I'm—" I watched Mack's beautiful face fade from neutral to infuriated, laced with a bit of terror.

His Adam's apple bobbed. "Yes, I'll be right there." He ended the call. "King is with Theodora. He says he wants to talk."

"Fuck." *Bad to worse to hell.*

"I have to go." Mack stormed toward the front door.

"I'm coming with you."

"No. You're staying right here. You and that ink are the only things that can keep Theodora and me alive."

CHAPTER TWELVE

Mack called me from his car on the way to the hotel and told me I was to listen closely. If he gave the word, I was to write the final letter on the paper. If the line cut or I stopped hearing anything, I was to write that final letter. Basically, take no chances. Kill King unless we got his compliance.

Ten minutes passed as I sat there on my couch, listening to the rumble of Mack's Ferrari and the noise of traffic. In my shaking hand, I held the pen inked and ready to go. Sweat trickled down my spine, and my eyes kept blurring from the tears I willed away. I held King's life in my hands and, even though I knew this man wasn't really him, part of me still wanted to cling to the hope that there was a way. A miracle waiting to happen. But my mind argued back.

You have to do this, Mia. You have to.

I suddenly heard heavy footsteps and then the creak of a door opening.

"King, so nice to see you," said Mack. "Now let Theodora leave. You and I can resolve this on our own."

I heard King's sadistic laugh. "Oh, we sure as hell will, my brother." The cell phone went dead.

"What? No, no, no. Fuck." I picked up the phone and looked at the screen that read Call Ended.

I threw back my head. *Shit. Shit. What do I do?*

If I called back, it would only waste time. King could be killing them right now!

My hand shook with fear. My body went cold and numb, but my heart felt like it was being pushed through a sieve. Painful. It didn't want to go to the place it needed to.

But Mack had been clear, and I couldn't argue. If anything happened, anything at all, I had to do it.

"I love you, King." I started to cry and carefully scripted a G onto the paper. I then set down the pen. I felt like I'd lost him all over again. Why did it all have to end like this? What was the purpose of everything we'd all gone through?

This just wasn't fair. It wasn't.

My phone rang like a siren of doom. I slowly reached out my hand and pushed the speaker. "Hello?"

"Mia, it's Teddi," she said, her voice high pitched and quivering.

"What happened?"

"I don't know. King grabbed me. Mack lunged for him and then collapsed. Mack's on the floor and King disappeared."

I pushed my lids closed and tilted my head toward the ceiling. *Shit. Shit. Shit.* King took Mack out before I could get him.

"He's still breathing, but he's unconscious," Teddi added, her voice hysterical.

"What?" I whooshed out a breath. "I'll be right there. Don't move."

I jerked up from the sofa and eyed the tiny bottle of ink. It would be safer here, but what if I needed it? What if King wasn't gone?

No. That didn't make any sense. If King was still alive, if that was what I could call him, the ink hadn't worked.

I grabbed the paper, ink, and pen and scrambled upstairs, depositing them carefully into the safe in my closet. It was late and Arch and Ypirétria were sound asleep, so I left a note. Arno could translate it for her since I couldn't write in Greek and she couldn't read or speak English.

I ran to the six-car garage and grabbed the first vehicle. King's sleek black Mercedes—one of many he owned—and I hit the road.

Ten minutes later, I pulled up to the hotel's palm-tree-lined circular driveway and realized I had no idea what room Teddi was in. I handed the car over to the valet and sprinted into the lobby. Teddi didn't answer her phone, which sent my heart into another tailspin.

"Hi, I'm looking for...for...Theodora and Mack Minos," I said to the receptionist.

"I'm sorry, ma'am, but we cannot give out guests' room numbers. You can call them on the house phone, if you like."

"It's an emergency."

The woman picked up the phone, and I reached across the counter to push down the receiver.

"What room?" I growled.

The woman was about to say something that I assumed would come from a can of on-the-job-training bullcrap.

I leaned in. "Listen to me, honey. If you do not give me that room number, I will hop over that counter and beat it out of you. And trust me, the police won't do shit because even the Spiros know not to fuck with me. Got it?"

It was the one advantage of having the Spiros loyal to me. Half of them were police. The other half owned a hundred different businesses or held positions in the local government on this island.

She pointed to her right. "They are in the presidential suite."

I rolled my eyes. Of course they were.

She continued, "Take the elevator to the top floor and go left to the end of the hall."

"Thank you." I ran as fast as I could, skipping the elevator and taking the stairs up to the fifth floor. This hotel was really a beachside resort, with cabanas, villas and suites.

I got to the suite and tapped on the door.

Teddi answered right away. "It all happened so

fast." She sniffled, her face raw with tears.

I stormed inside and immediately spotted Mack lying on the ground. Other than that, nothing was broken or out of place. "Has he moved?"

"No." She shook her head. "And his pulse is rapid."

I leaned over him, feeling his warm breath on my cheek. King might not have had time to kill Mack, but he'd done something to him.

"I told Mack this was a mistake coming here," she whimpered. "I told him to just end King while we had a chance."

I stood up and took her hand. "I know how you're feeling right now. I really do. But we have to think. Are you sure King is gone?"

She looked away from the disturbing scene before us, toward the open window. "I don't know. I saw him swing for Mack and then his hand just sort of passed through him. King looked confused, and then he wrapped his arms around Mack's neck and began tugging, like he was trying to grab onto him. Then Mack just fell to the floor."

Oh my God. "This is so fucking awful." I needed to think. Without Mack, we were dead in the water. And poor Teddi. I knew how she felt. I felt the same. But we couldn't afford to just sit and do nothing.

"Let's get Mack up on the bed." I took his arms, and she took his feet. Like King, Mack was a big guy. Six three. Lean solid muscle. Broad shoulders.

They weren't meaty men, but they were strong and weighed a ton.

Between the two of us, we managed to get him up on the bed just before there was a knock on the door.

"Let me," I said and went over to check the peephole. A robust-looking security guard stood there with an intimidating scowl.

Great.

I opened the door. "Everything's fine here and you can tell the receptionist downstairs—"

"Mrs. Minos, we just wanted to be sure you're all right."

I noticed his name tag had the word *Spiros* written on it.

"The receptionist is my cousin," he said.

"Oh. I'm so sorry. I wouldn't really have hurt her," I lied. I so would've kicked the hell out of her if I'd had to.

"So everything's fine?" he asked.

"Yes. Thank you. All good."

"I'll just be standing out here until Arno gets here."

Oh no. Arno. I hadn't called him to tell him what was going on. He would not be happy.

"Thank you." I shut the door and turned toward Teddi, who just stood there with her mouth hanging open, her face as pale as a sheet of paper. My eyes followed hers toward the bed.

Mack sat up, glaring at her with such a vicious

scowl it took me a moment to realize.

"Fuck. That's not Mack, is it?" I whispered.

She shook her head no.

Christ almighty. I guess now we know why King was tugging on Mack. He was throwing him out of his body.

"Well, well, well, Ms. Turner." King turned his hateful gaze toward mine. "Aren't you full of surprises?"

"But you…you weren't supposed to…"

"Live? Oh, don't worry. I'm going to die. That you may be sure of. But I think you forgot one important thing: Mack has been living in *my* body. You've killed us both."

CHAPTER THIRTEEN

It took Teddi and me several moments of standing there to fully absorb the horror and comprehend the missing piece to all this—what really happened the day that King resurrected Mack. Teddi had been there, and she said that King had simply vanished into the ground. Then Mack appeared in his old body, the one he'd been born with.

Wrong.

We hadn't seen the truth because no one had questioned the mechanics. I had been out of my mind with grief, too devastated from losing my husband. Teddi had been too focused on the miracle before her. And neither of us connected that event to King's recent activity of grabbing warm living bodies for his dead, newly resurrected buddies. We simply hadn't seen it: The soul needed somewhere to go. And when King used the chalice on Mack, he had given up his body for his brother.

"Why the hell would King do this?" Teddi whispered under her breath, trying her best to keep from falling apart.

I wished I knew. I truly did. Because if King had seen this all coming, then it meant he knew the ink would take Mack down with him. *It kills the body and the soul.*

Oh God. If I was right, that meant if it came down to our lives versus King's and Mack's, King wanted us to live. King *had* chosen me—us—over his brother. He likely had hoped, however, that he could keep us all alive, that it would not come to this.

It was a bittersweet moment.

I went to the little sitting area by the door and dropped down, the tears forming in my eyes.

Teddi sat beside me, her eyes glazed over and face lacking any emotion. She was in shock. So was I.

"He's dying," she whispered, giving my hand a light squeeze.

I across the room at the man lying on the bed, trying to make out the details of King's ethereal beauty through the blur of salty tears screaming from my face. I pressed the moisture from my eyes with my palms and wiped them on the back of my jeans. King's face grew paler by the second. His eyes were closed and breathing rapid.

I couldn't focus. I couldn't put the pieces together inside my head of what to do. The blow was just too much. Losing King. Losing Mack. Knowing King did love us enough to give up someone he held so dear.

It was all too much.

"You have to ask him, Mia," Teddi whispered. "You have to try. Even if you have to lie."

I stared into her bloodshot green eyes, hearing her, not hearing her.

"Mia," she hiccupped down a breath, "you have to try. I can't know that Mack died for nothing. You can't do that to me."

I shook my head. So much confusion. "I don't understand."

"The names, Mia. Get the names. And do it quickly."

Names, names. She wanted names. "What names?"

"10 Club."

Oh. Them. They didn't feel real. None of this did. I felt numb from head to toe.

I looked across the hotel room at the man in the bed, his face nearly lifeless, and rallied the will to stand. One step, then another, and I was kneeling next to him, pressing his cold hand to my cheek.

"I will never understand any of this, King, but if you can hear me—the real you—I just want you to know I forgive you." It was painful and horrific, but I was suddenly thinking about what I might do to save him or my children. Would I sleep with someone if it meant saving their lives?

Yes.

I would.

I would give everything I had—my life, my

soul, my body—in a heartbeat. *Damn you, King.* I finally understood what he'd done. He'd used everything in his power, even his body, to try to save someone he loved with all his heart. There wasn't a piece of himself he wouldn't sacrifice for us, and I could no longer hold his infidelity against him. Nor could I blame him for abandoning us or the fact he'd come back so broken. Because now I knew, without a doubt, that none of this had been the desired outcome. *But you knew you would have to give up everything to try to save Mack, didn't you, King?* However, King also knew himself. He'd acquired so much knowledge and power over thousands of years, he probably feared he might not stay dead. And if he'd had to trade his soul for Mack's, he knew he'd return as a monster. So King had made sure there was some sort of fail-safe if the worst came to be. *The ink.* In short, King had been willing to give his own life for Mack's, but not ours.

"I love you," I whispered, holding his hand to my cheek. "And if you're still in there somewhere fighting, I need your help. We need to know the names to put on the list, King."

He coughed and wheezed, his blue eyes slitting open. "I am touched, Ms. Turner. Truly," he mumbled. "But it is as I told you. That man is gone."

I looked into his eyes. "You're not coming back this time, King. Why not just help me? Why not help your son and your daughter? Because 10 Club will take her the moment she's born; some sadistic man will make her his slave or worse. You can't possibly want that for her."

King smiled weakly. "If they're truly my children, fear will make them strong, and they will rise to the top."

I felt my blood sour in horror. "No. No, they'll live tormented lives. They'll become like you—if they survive."

King opened his eyes wide and alert. "I always believed a little darkness is healthy in a person. Good for the soul."

I dropped my forehead to his hand. "What you've created isn't a little darkness. It's so much worse. Why would you want this?"

"It is," he said with a breathy voice, "as I told you. Power is everything. And I am through living like a cockroach in the shadows. I am a king. A powerful king born to rule, and all I needed was the right army."

I lifted my head and tilted it to the side. "You wanted to be king of…everyone?"

He smiled lopsidedly. "People are savages, Ms. Turner. Simply look at this world—the mass killings over oil, rape, genocide, corruption. What the world needs is a cruel hand to keep it in check."

So that was his plan? Resurrect the most powerful people he'd ever known, use some sort of magic to make them all loyal to him—like he'd done with the Spiros—and then be king again.

"You're out of your mind," I whispered.

"Am I?" he replied in a slow voice, his breathing labored. "10 Club already runs this world. I merely proposed to bring them into the light and make it official. With my people at the helm, of course."

"Who are your people, King? Give me the names."

"Talia, I've only got a minute. You are to take over as planned."

Talia? That was when I noticed he wasn't talking to me. He had a cell in his hand. It had to be from Mack's pocket. He must've dialed when I had my head down.

"Shit!" I snatched the device away right as Talia's voice came over the speaker.

"I will find a way to bring you back, King," Talia said.

"What? No!" I gasped.

"Is that bitch there with you?" she said. "Tell her I'm coming for her."

I ended the call and chucked the phone against the wall. "Goddammit! Why would you do that?"

King flashed a weak, but sadistic grin. "Because I never give up. And Talia won't either." The light faded from his eyes.

"No," I muttered in horror. "No! No. You can't do this!" I pounded on his chest. "Give me the names, for fuck's sake," I screamed, crying. "You can't do this to us!"

"Mia." I felt a gentle tug on my arm, but the

emotions had hold of me now, the images of the torture and torment my children would endure.

"No!" I pushed her back and straddled him, beating his chest. "You can't do this!"

"He's gone, Mia. We lost." Teddi cried hysterically.

"No…" I rested my forehead on his chest and sobbed. "Please God. Don't do this to us."

Sadly, no one was listening. King was dead. Mack was dead. And 10 Club was alive. With fucking Talia at the helm. *Oh God.*

CHAPTER FOURTEEN

I don't remember Arno arriving to the hotel room. I don't remember them taking the body away to be buried for the second time in the king's sacred tomb, wherever the hell that was. I don't remember Teddi coming home with me. I don't remember eating or drinking or pissing or breathing or anything.

My mind was consumed by the most horrific darkness imaginable. Devastation was five steps up from where I lived.

The most powerful, evil people ever to cross King's path were now free, alive, and working as a team under the world's most sadistic bitch. In some ways, Talia was worse than King because she enjoyed killing just for fun. King always had a reason for everything he did, even if they weren't nice reasons. But Talia, who had been King's partner of sorts before I came along, had been obsessed with him. I suspected that was why he handed over 10 Club to her. She wouldn't rest until she brought King back, and she would rule 10 Club with an iron fist.

And soon, 10 Club will come for me. They would come for Teddi and Arch, too.

Worst of all, the pain of losing King had been reignited. I could no longer shield my grief with bitterness and anger. The man I loved did everything he could to save his brother and keep us all safe. He cared nothing for himself or his own happiness. We were all that mattered.

I got up from bed and glanced at the clock on the nightstand. *Three a.m.*

I went to Arch's room, next to mine, and found the crib empty. I stumbled my way down the hall to Ypirétria's room, but found Teddi curled up in her bed instead. She had her arms wrapped around Arch. A box of spent tissues lay on the nightstand alongside piles of crumpled wads flowing onto the floor.

I sighed. "I'm so sorry, Theodora." She was pregnant and had lost a man that she'd been born to love. And thanks to me, she was now alone. I'd put that nail in Mack's coffin. I should've seen what would happen.

I slid into bed, putting Arch between us. The light in the hallway shined on his pouty little lips, catching the lines of his thick black lashes fanning across his chubby cheeks. I slid my palm over his stomach. "I love you, little guy."

"You're awake." Teddi looked at me with those stunning green eyes.

"I don't know. Am I?" I went back to stroking Arch's little stomach.

"He was crying. He misses you."

"I missed him, too." Even if I hadn't been lucid. "How many hours was I out?"

"You were gone for over a day."

That took a moment to sink in. "How's that possible?"

"You were inconsolable. We had to sedate you."

"Oh."

"I wouldn't let them drug you tonight, though," she said.

"Do I want to know why?" I whispered.

"Arno said he heard rumors around town of a big party at King's place tonight. People are flying in from all over. Important people."

Oh fuck. A 10 Club gathering. "We have to leave here."

"That's the problem," she said. "There isn't a safer place."

I nodded solemnly. She was right. King had done everything possible to make this a fortress where "bad things" couldn't enter. That said, "Sooner or later we'll have to leave. We can't live in here forever."

"I know," she said. "So what are we going to do, Mia?"

Her question wasn't rhetorical. She looked to me for the answer. I was the only way she could see out.

I rolled on to my back and stared at the ceiling. I had nothing.

"Please, Mia. Mack and King are gone. They're not coming back, and I don't know anything about Seers or 10 Club or how to get out of this. But you do. You have to know of something we can do."

"I don't." I let out a breath. "I'm so sorry, but I don't know." I wished I did.

"Mia." She sat up and crossed her legs. "If you even think of giving up, I will rip out your goddamned eyes. You can't let me die. You can't let Mack's baby die. You can't let your entire family go out like this."

I covered my eyes with my arm, but didn't speak.

"Please, Mia. Whatever possibility there is not to be raped, tortured, murdered, and not to watch our children die, you have to do it. Just tell me what to do."

I scrubbed my mind, trying to ignore the throbbing heartache in my chest. "I'm sorry. I can't." I got up from the bed and scooped up Arch, intending to tuck him back in his crib.

Teddi dashed to the doorway and held out her arm. "I refuse to let it end here, Mia. I fucking refuse."

"I don't know what to do, Teddi. If we run, they'll track us down. If we fight, we'll lose. There are too many of them." King had been right; the only thing that mattered was power. *If you happen to enjoy staying alive.*

"Try fucking harder," she snarled. "Think. Think about anything King told you, anything you saw or learned or…anything to end them."

I had tried. A million times I'd thought about how to kill them off. The problem was they had eyes and ears everywhere. There wasn't a country or government agency they didn't have their claws into. I'd even seen A-list actors at 10 Club parties. *They're like a giant cancer.*

"Wait." My eyes locked with hers as I swayed Arch in my arms.

"What?"

"I don't know—I mean, it probably won't work, but it might."

"What?" she snapped, making Arch squirm and whimper.

I started bouncing him gently in my arms. "They're like an illness. One big organism."

"And?" she said.

"Mack said we need names, but what if we don't? What if the only thing we need to write with that ink is '10 Club'?"

She blinked at me. "It can't be that easy."

A loud thump on the front door made us both jump. Suddenly, the house exploded with loud noises—windows breaking, doors falling, men screaming.

"They're here, Mia! How did they get in?" Teddi shrieked.

"I don't know." I took a breath as Arch wailed.

"Where's the ink?" she asked.

I jerked my head to the left. "In the safe." She scrambled behind me as I made my way through my bedroom to the walk-in closet. "Take him." I handed off Arch, who screamed like a banshee. My trembling hands punched in the code, and somewhere in the back of my mind I heard them coming. 10 Club slaves, Talia, Hagne, I didn't know. But they were here for us.

How had they gotten in?

The safe popped open just as gunshots thundered inside the house.

Fuck. Fuck! I could only hope the bullets had come from the Spiros's side of the fight.

"Hurry, Mia. Hurry!" Teddi squealed as quietly as a person who was about to die could.

My shaking hands pulled the paper, pen, and ink from the safe. "Go close the bedroom door and lock it," I commanded. It would buy us two seconds, and I'd take what I could get.

Teddi did what I asked, and I got to my knees, spreading out the paper. I uncorked the tiny bottle and dipped the pen, knocking the ink over in the process.

"Shit. No, no, no." I saturated the tip with what I could and went to writing.

10 Club.

I looked up at Teddi and nodded. "It's done."

A loud pounding on the door halted our breathing.

"We don't have enough time. They'll get inside before it works." Teddi clutched Arch to her chest.

"Mia! I can hear you in there, you fucking cunt!" screamed Hagne. "Get out here!"

Jesus. Hagne. Now she worked for Talia and there would be nothing to hold her back from hurting me in the worst way possible.

"We need more time," Teddi whispered, trying to calm Arch.

I looked at Teddi and my baby cradled in her arms. I had to do something. But what? The ink drying on that paper was our only hope, but it had taken King twenty minutes or more to die.

I slid the paper into my safe and locked it. At least it couldn't be destroyed.

"Mia, hurry. Think of something. Do you have a gun or—or anything?"

"No." I hadn't wanted them around the house. Only the Spiros were allowed to carry weapons. King's insistence.

My mind spun faster and faster.

Then the doorjamb splintered as they rammed inside.

Time's up.

જ્જ જ્

"Who's the little bitch now, huh, Mia?" Hagne watched with a wide smile in her hateful blue eyes from the corner of my bedroom as a group of armed men dragged us out. There were no words when I had to step over Ypirétria's body lying facedown in a pool of blood in the hallway. They'd shot her in the back.

I couldn't bear to look. *I'm going to lose it. Just...fucking lose it.* Ypirétria hadn't been a threat to anyone. She was an old woman who loved children and cooking. *Motherfuckers.*

Fearing for Arch's, my, and Teddi's lives, I had to keep my mouth shut and say nothing to provoke Hagne.

The men took us outside, where Arno and two other Spiros men lay dead in the driveway next to a black van. They died trying to protect us, and it wrenched my heart.

Twenty minutes for the ink to work. That's all we need. And this island, likely unbeknownst to 10 Club, was filled with Spiros. All loyal to me. They would be coming after them.

Once inside the van, seated on the floor in the back with one of the men pointing a gun at us, I began counting in my head as the minutes passed. It would take us ten or fifteen minutes to get to King's house. Then I would need to stall for time. If it came down to it, I would run or make a scene or do anything I could to drag out the minutes and allow Arch and Teddi to live.

I looked at Teddi's puffy eyes. She still held a screaming Arch, who was not at all happy.

From the passenger seat, Hagne turned around. "Shut that little fucker up, Mia. Or I'll have them put a bullet in his head."

White-hot rage dotted my vision. Yes, I doubted she'd kill Arch—he was too valuable—but the threat was enough to set me off. Still, I had to stay calm.

I cleared my throat. "He's King's son. He's not a fan of following instructions."

Hagne cackled. "Yes. Well, I'm sure it will only add to his value when we auction him off tonight."

"You can't do that, Hagne," I growled.

"If you haven't noticed, I can do anything I like. King is no longer in charge, Mia."

"He might come back. And then what happens?" I asked.

She laughed toward the ceiling of the van and the lights of a passing car caught the highlights of her golden hair. Hair so much like mine. It fucking chaffed me that he'd chosen a body that looked like mine. Like some evil twin.

"King is not coming back. Not this time. Talia is delusional," she scoffed.

"Don't be so sure. He's returned from worse."

She turned and looked at me again. "Really? Then why have his wards weakened? It's because he's gone. Gone gone. Whatever was left of that soul of his crossed over." She turned back around and faced the road. "Evil bastard. Good riddance."

I wanted to tell her to shut the hell up, that all this was her fault. She'd been the one who started the issues with King and the Seers so many thousands of years ago. It had been her greedy, selfish black heart.

I hope you rot in fucking hell, Hagne.

When we pulled up to King's historic hillside home, there was in fact a very large party in full swing. People in expensive evening wear—ball gowns, tuxedos, and expensive-looking jewelry—congregated outside. *Great. It's the evil Oscars.*

The men escorted Teddi and me inside. We still wore our pajamas and looked like hell from grieving all day. The people smirked and laughed as they made way to let us inside.

"Take them out back. I'll go get Talia." Hagne disappeared into the gawking crowd. So many faces seemed familiar, but my mind stayed focused on counting down the minutes.

"Fourteen," I said to Teddi, who walked slowly, her face lacking any emotion.

She handed me Arch. "It will work. It has to."

The men took us outside to a large terrace with tables, white linens, and candles. It looked like a goddamned wedding. Only it was three in the morning and we were about to be sold off or tortured or something. *Not very wedding-like entertainment.*

The men walked us over to an elevated arbor and made us stand facing the guests, who now congregated around us.

"My dear guests! Can I get everyone's attention,

please?" Talia strolled outside wearing a tight green dress. She wore her brown hair in a twist and had on a ton of makeup. She looked like a hooker.

She stood in front of the crowd with her back to us. "Ladies and gentlemen, tonight, as new president of 10 Club, it is my honor to present to you the two individuals responsible for the death of King, a beloved member of our esteemed group."

What a sham. They loved no one. They cared for no one. And he'd been way more than a simple member.

I glanced at Teddi nervously. We had to be coming up on twenty minutes, but everyone looked fine. Better than fine.

Talia continued, "So in accordance with the rules of 10 Club, King's possessions now belong to his wife."

The crowd booed and gave the thumbs-down.

Where the hell is she going with this?

"Now, now," Talia laughed, "but we all know that it does not end there. As his wife, Mia here is responsible for his debts." She turned to me. "So, Mia, are you prepared to settle King's unpaid debts?"

"What are you talking about?"

"Well," she smiled, "King has to pay his dues like anyone else and I'm afraid his membership came up for renewal last week."

This is ridiculous.

"Oh no," she said, "from the look on your face,

I'm guessing you don't have a billion dollars handy." She made a pouty face. "Such a shame because that means you and your possessions, including your little baby, are now property of 10 Club." She turned back to the crowd. "Looks like we'll be having an auction tonight, people!"

The crowd applauded.

Hagne's face, toward the front of the crowd, beamed with joy. "I offer two million for the baby!"

"What?" I stepped back, only to feel the cold barrel of a gun pointed at my back. "No. You can't fucking have him." I looked at Teddi.

"It's been twenty minutes, Mia. Why hasn't it worked?" she said.

"I don't know!"

Talia raised her voice over the rumble of the excited guests. "We have two million! Do we have three? I understand the child has Seer blood."

"Five million!" another man barked out.

No. No. Fuck no. I would not let them auction off my son like a goddamned mystical cow. I would not let this happen.

"Five million going once. Going twice."

"Ten million!" Hagne barked out. Where the hell did she get that kind of money? *Probably evil King gave it to her.*

"Ten. We have ten. Anyone else?"

The crowd remained silent.

"Sold!" Talia screamed and pointed at Hagne.

The man behind me came around and started

trying to pry Arch from my arms. "Get the fuck away from me."

Arch cried hysterically and Teddi jumped in, trying to help.

Just then, we heard a scream off in the distance. Then another.

I didn't know if by some miracle the ink had worked or the Spiros had come to help us, but I took Teddi's hand. "Run!"

We darted through the worried-looking crowd, who paid us no attention. We were nothing to them and certainly no threat. But people like these had tons of enemies, though most were each other.

We pushed past more party guests and made our way into King's study. I locked the door behind us.

"Fuck, Mia! What's happening?" Teddi panted.

More screams echoed through the home and outside toward the front. "It could be the Spiros or the ink or…someone attacking the guests. I don't know."

We suddenly heard a grunt and thud against the wall, like two people fighting just outside the door.

"Get the fuck off me!" we heard Hagne roar.

"Where are they?" a man grumbled.

"Dead. Like you," Hagne barked.

A crunching sound, followed by a low gurgle, made my skin crawl. Whoever he'd been, Hagne had just taken him out. At least, that was my best guess.

"Is it the Spiros? It has to be, right?" Teddi whispered frantically.

"I'm not sure, but yes. Yes, it's probably them." Still, it didn't sound like they were winning. "And I don't think the ink worked." Hagne would be dead by now.

"They won, Mia. They won." Teddi placed her hands over her stomach protectively. "People like us can't stop them. We're too weak."

"We'll find another way." Because giving up wasn't an option.

I squinted, my eyes tearing like hell and my body shaking like an adrenaline-pumped leaf. We had to get somewhere safe. Safe and away from 10 Club. Somewhere they couldn't find us. Because they would never stop hunting us. We'd never be safe as long as they were alive.

"Mia!" Teddi barked.

I opened my eyes. Teddi stared at my stomach. I glanced down and saw a light. Instinctually, I reached out and grabbed Teddi's hand.

❧ ❧

"Mia? Mia? Wake up, Mia. Where the fuck are we?" Teddi's sweet voice echoed in the back of my mind, but felt unreachable.

I cracked open my lids to find her green eyes hovering over me. The sound of crashing waves and men's voices yelling off in the distance sieved into my ears.

"Mia?" She slapped my cheek hard.

"Ow." I groaned, putting my hand over the stinging skin. "Teddi?"

"Mia." Her nostrils flared. "Please tell me you know what the hell is going on."

Slowly, I sat up, feeling the gritty sand sticking to my arms. I had Arch clutched to my chest, wailing. I looked around at the pristine white sand, the hot sun above, and the shirtless men with swords drawn and charging toward us.

I let out something that was between a sigh of relief and nervous sobs.

"Mia?" Teddi shrieked.

"It's okay, Teddi. Just stay calm. We'll be okay."

She stared at me like I'd lost my fucking marbles as the men came up on us.

I kissed the top of Arch's head and closed my eyes. "We're safe now," I whispered. "I promise. We're safe."

CHAPTER FIFTEEN

The men, who'd never seen a woman with blonde hair, pajama bottoms, T-shirts, or Arch's diapers and onesie, led us toward the temples I'd seen only a few times but dreamt of on a hundred occasions. They were rectangular with high ceilings and stone pillars, painted in elaborate blue and red murals depicting people fishing or offering grains and fruit to the gods.

"Just stay calm," I assured Teddi, whose sheet-white face was covered in sweat. Her brown hair had sand stuck to it, and her clothes were wet with salt water on one side. She must've "landed" in the water. I was sure I didn't look so hot either in my pink PJs.

"What's happening?" she hissed.

"I think it was the baby." I pressed my hand to my stomach. "She helped us." Or something like that. I didn't really know much other than she was powerful and her blood ran through mine.

"Move it." A man with a sword pushed me up the stone steps of the temple, through the main doorway, and placed us behind a crowd of people dressed in everything from rags to neatly pleated gowns or skirts for the men.

"Mia," Teddi whispered, staring at the stunning, shirtless figure with long black hair and a short dark beard seated on a low platform ahead of us, "please tell me we're dreaming."

"We're not."

Being taller than the people in front of us, our voices caught his attention immediately.

Blue, blue eyes locked onto my face.

"Dear God. That's King, isn't it?" Teddi mumbled.

I nodded, soaking him in. *King. Alive.* My heart accelerated to hummingbird speed. "Just stay calm."

"For fuck's sake, Mia, what have you done?"

I turned to Teddi, trying to calm poor little Arch, who now roared and hiccupped, snot and tears flying everywhere. "Mack is here, too, Teddi. They both are."

She covered her mouth and then dropped to her hands and knees and threw up. From the corner of my eye, I saw King storming toward us, pushing the crowd to the sides. I watched with bated breath as he stopped just a few feet away. I never thought I'd see him again, and it took everything I had not to throw my arms around him and weep. Or drop to my knees and barf in hysterics like Teddi.

"Who are you? And what in the gods' names are you doing on our island?"

I took a deep breath and stared up at him. *Oh, hell.* I threw my arm around him, sandwiching Arch between us. He smelled so good—sweet and citrusy mixed with exotic herbs. "I missed you so much."

King pushed us away and stared into my eyes with confusion. He then looked at the screaming baby in my arms and at me again. "Who are you?"

I composed myself as best as I could. "My name is Mia, and this is Archon." I placed my hand on my stomach. "And she is Ariadna. We've come a long, long way to see you again."

He scratched the back of his head, frowning at my face like he knew us but wasn't sure from where.

"Get that one off the floor," he commanded me, and then addressed the guard standing behind us. "Take them to my private chamber. Don't let them go anywhere or speak to anyone."

I tried to help a hysterical Teddi from the stone floor while keeping a firm grip on Arch. It wasn't easy. She'd reached her breaking point. I was pretty darn close myself.

"We need Mack to come, too," I said.

King gave me a look.

"I meant Callias. We have to see him. Ask him to come, too."

"Why would I do that, woman?"

"Because you're both the reason we're here, and we can't fuck it up this time."

࿐ ࿐

The shirtless guards with braided dark hair, wearing pleated blue skirts, escorted us to a ten-by-ten room that I knew wasn't King's private chamber. In our modern terms, it was more like his office, with a small table, a few wooden stools, and a few rolled-up animal hides sitting on stone shelves. No door. I didn't think they'd been invented here yet, though they did use cloth during the colder days, according to King. Off in the distance, beyond the courtyard, seagulls circled above and the sound of waves roared. This spot wasn't very far from the location of our modern-day palace.

Before the guards exited the room, I asked their names. Spiros. Both of them.

Thank God. "Can you please bring us boiled water, some boiled goat milk, and one of those leather bags you use to carry water?"

The two men stared like I'd lost my ever-loving marbles, but were they compelled to help me?

"I insist," I said.

The taller man jerked his head, indicating the other one should do as I asked. "I'll stay here."

"Thank you." It seemed that whatever spell or magic King had used to make the Spiros bloodline loyal to me had remained intact. Or maybe they were simply being nice. Either way, we were grateful. Especially Arch. I hadn't been breast-feeding him regularly since King died—hadn't had the strength—so I gave him what I had and then used the leather pouch to feed him the warm goat milk. It went everywhere, but enough got inside his belly to put him to sleep.

"That's not going to cut it, Mia."

"I know. I'll have to figure out something better later." After all, I wasn't the only woman with a baby in these times. They had to do something for diapers, cribs, and baby food.

"This can't be happening," Teddi said, pacing the short distance of the room, alternating between tears and mild hysterics.

"I don't get it. You're a three-thousand-year-old Seer. You lived in the times of the Mayans and died and came back to life and died again. Why is this so hard for you to accept?"

She snapped her head in my direction. "I don't remember my past lives. And for fuck's sake! I never moved backwards in time, Mia. We can't be here. It's impossible. And then what happens if Mack's life turns out differently and our paths don't cross again? What happens to my baby? What about you, Mia? What happens to Arch and your baby if you change everything?"

"I don't know, Teddi. But what did you want me to do? Let Hagne break into the room and slit our throats? I didn't have a choice. The ink didn't work. So now we're here. Now we live another day and we figure it the fuck out." Personally, as scared as I felt, knowing King was here—alive and good— gave me a sort of peace I hadn't known since this all started. I'd completely given up all hope. *But he's alive.*

She clenched her eyes shut. "Okay. Okay. You're right."

A slender young woman with dark skin and long black hair appeared in the doorway. "The king will see you now."

Teddi and I exchanged nervous glances.

"I don't know what I'll do when I see Mack," Teddi said.

I understood. I really did. These were the men we loved, but we were strangers to them.

I gently repositioned Arch on my chest. "Just take it slow. Give them time to digest it all."

"What if they think we're just two crazy women from another country or tribe or whatever?"

"They're not like that in these times. They believe in the impossible."

We followed the woman outside, where two shirtless guards in blue skirts showed us through a courtyard with potted flowers. They led us into a large banquet room with arched doorways and murals of fruit trees covering the walls. Six women with dark features and long hair sat around the table lit with oil bowls in the middle. One more woman with silver hair, who looked to be very old, sat at the end of the table.

They're Seers. I knew because the entire room buzzed with energy.

King, who stood at the middle of the long stone table, gestured for us to sit across from him.

I remained calm and clearheaded. I couldn't fuck this up. I had to make sure I took control of the situation and made our fates different. That was not what happened last time when I'd managed to repeat history and change nothing—King getting cursed, Justin dying, the 10 Club being created.

"You." King pointed to me. "Your clothing and manner of speech tell me you are not from anywhere we are familiar with. So tell us who sent you."

All righty. I looked around the table, hugging my sleeping baby. "My name is Mia and this is not the first time I've been here."

It took almost an hour to tell the watered-down story of how I met King—a ghost of an ancient cursed king looking for salvation—of how tormented and evil he was, and how I'd come to this period in time to escape his cruelty but also looking for him—the real him, wanting to undo whatever horrible things had been done to him. I told them how King had a journal that told the story of Hagne, Mack, and himself. Of how Hagne wanted King dead because she loved Mack. She then used her powers to seduce him and convince him to challenge King for power. Then I came here and thought I would change our futures.

"It didn't work," I said. "I changed nothing."

King chuckled. "You truly think any of us believe your wild tale?"

I looked down at my bare feet. "I do not."

"Mia," Teddi asked in English, which they

could not understand, "what is he saying? It doesn't sound good—"

"Leave us." The silver-haired woman at the farthest end of the table nodded to the guards, who came forward to take us back to the room.

"I need a place to lie down," I said.

"You can go lie with the slaves. That is generosity enough for someone like you," King growled.

I shot him a look. They did not treat their slaves exceptionally horrible, but they didn't treat them like regular people either.

"I'm not subjecting our child to those conditions." Conditions I would love to change if ever in a position to do so.

"Take them to your guest chamber," said the old woman.

That was the room next to his, overlooking his favorite beach. To the side of that was an orchard and flower garden. It was the exact spot where our house stood today.

"This dirty, vile little gipsy woman with her mutt will not stay there. I am the king and no one tells me—"

"I am your *wife*." I scowled.

He leaned into the table with fists planted. "You are a crazy witch who will be executed if she speaks out of turn again."

Teddi pulled me back. "Mia, get a hold of yourself."

She didn't understand anything we were saying,

but she knew how emotionally tapped I felt. We'd both been through hell.

"Yes, you're right," I said to her. "I'm just tired."

"I know. So am I. We need to rest."

I looked at King. "We don't want to make any trouble. We'll stay wherever you like."

"There's a nice fishing boat with holes on the other side of the island." King flashed a cruel little smile.

Wow. He was really being a dick. And he definitely didn't seem to want anything to do with me.

I bowed my head begrudgingly. "Wherever the king sees fit to put us."

"What did he say?" Teddi asked.

"We really need to get you one of these." I lifted my sleeve and showed her my tattoo. It was the one Hagne had given me during my last visit. I hated her. I hated that she'd made a mark on my body, but I couldn't deny the power was amazing.

"What is that?" asked one of the women who sat closest to our side of the table.

The silver-haired woman at the end popped up from the table with a spryness that didn't seem to fit her age. "How did you get that?"

"Hagne gave it to me the last time I was here," I replied.

"But I have not yet taught her this spell."

I shrugged. "But obviously you will. She made it with a quill, some spit, and something she chewed up from a little pouch."

The woman's eyes went wide. "You may go now. We have much to discuss."

I felt King's hateful gaze on me as Teddi and I followed the two shirtless men out of the inner compound to a shabbier-looking cluster of buildings—no decorative paint on the walls, no potted fruit trees.

Slaves' quarters.

Teddi and I were put in a doorless room with one stone platform covered with hay for a bed and a clay jar on the floor.

Nice. It's our toilet.

"Well, I guess it's better than a sinking boat," I said.

"Or a house filled with 10 Club members," Teddi added.

Yes, at least there was that.

CHAPTER SIXTEEN

Teddi and I were not awake long, nor did we come close to getting enough sleep. Approximately three hours after being thrown in this room, just after sunset, another young woman came and brought us warm water and rags for bathing, beige linen tunics, and some long rectangular strips of cloth for Arch. I cleaned up Arch and folded the cloth into a diaper. I tucked the ends into his front since we were in the days before the invention of the safety pin. *Or baby bottles, formula, and disposable diapers. How did mothers survive?* At least for now, we were all clean and dry.

Immediately following, two other young women in long gray tunics showed up to do our hair. That was when I knew something was going down.

Ceremony was everything to these people—full moons, crop plantings, harvests, and honoring the gods on their special days. However, for their time, the Minoans were very advanced. They had beautiful pottery and metalworks, which they traded with foreigners as far away as China. They even had bathtubs and indoor plumbing. For the non-slaves, of course. *God, what I wouldn't give for a bath right now.*

Teddi's face turned red as the two young women tugged painfully at her brown hair, attempting to make elaborate twists and pin them on top with little metal clips adorned with tiny seashells. We both had shoulder-length bobs, so we looked like mops with lots of loose bits falling all around.

"It's okay," I told the girl. "Just leave it."

She didn't seem to like that idea because she'd been given an order by someone to make us look presentable. "You can't make a cake without flour," I told her. "No one will blame you."

The two ladies finished us by putting a dab of fragrant oil under our arms and then told us to follow. This time two guards, wearing blue and red skirts and feathered headbands, escorted us along. These were the king's special ceremonial guards.

They led us to the largest temple on the compound. I knew this was where King met with his council—the higher ranking families and Seers on the island.

We entered and the same women from earlier stood to one side of the towering room along with a horde of new faces. All women. All Seers. To the other side of the smoky, torchlit room, men dressed in neatly pleated skirts stood. King sat on his throne at the farthest end, wearing a bitter scowl on his handsome face. The moment he saw me, it turned into a pure loathing growl.

My heart sank. Why did he hate me so much? It wasn't like this before.

"This doesn't look good," Teddi whispered.

"I know. Just stay calm."

A young servant girl asked to take Arch, who still slept, but I refused. Like hell I'd be letting a stranger touch my baby.

The eldest Seer, the one who'd been speaking earlier, stepped forward and began addressing King.

"Due to the concerning nature of the matter brought to us by our guests, the Seers gathered earlier. We admit this is a situation we have never come across, but we have consulted with our ancestors and reached an agreement as to the best course of action."

King nodded with his bulky biceps crossed over his smooth, muscular chest. I tried not to look or think about how beautiful he looked, sitting there half-naked, displaying his ripped torso, a deep red cloth wrapped around his waist.

The Seer continued, "We believe that the gods are acting through these two strangers, who tell the truth. We believe that the one with the golden hair carries a child that is yours and that the infant is yours as well. The dark-haired one carries another Seer—a girl who is also very powerful and therefore not likely offspring to Callias. As we all know, the king has been blessed by the gods with extraordinary strength."

Uh-oh. What are they talking about? My mind sort of twirled around, scooping up facts. Teddi had conceived her after King brought Mack back to life. And if Mack lived inside King's body, then…well…biologically, they were right. Her baby wasn't Mack's. It was King's. If they were identical twins, would it really matter? *Other than they think King is stronger.* I suppose I couldn't argue. In any case, that made Teddi's baby a bigger target if we were to return home.

"What are they saying, Mia?" Teddi asked.

I glanced at Teddi. She did not need to hear that she wasn't really carrying Mack's baby. Besides, she was smart. She'd probably figure it out for herself one day.

"Umm…they believe us. Sort of. But they haven't gotten to their point yet," I said with a steady voice, wanting her to stay calm.

The elder woman raised her chin. "It is our opinion that time is of the essence, and we are not too late to appease the gods and change our fates. The king and his brother are to wed these two women."

"What?" King spat. "You are mad. I will not wed, and I will certainly not wed this outsider."

The silver-haired woman narrowed her dark eyes. I could tell from her body language and age that she didn't take lip from any man but did her best to remain respectful to her king.

She cleared her throat. "The gods clearly intended for you to be united with this woman one way or another. Otherwise, they would not have given her this gift of moving through time. And even after she lost her gift, they made it so her child would have it. Fate has spoken, my king, and you should listen."

King growled, and from the slight flare in his nostrils and the red on his sculpted cheekbones, I knew he was about to let loose.

She continued, "There are several other matters we must discuss, my king. Our ancestors made it clear that our fates, as the golden-haired one has told, are destined to repeat unless we create a new path forward. The challenge is that we are limited by this moment. Fate will not allow contradictions. We cannot create a future that makes this moment impossible."

"Can you say that in non-Seer speak?" I said.

She turned to me with a respectful nod. "The key events that brought you here to us in this moment must remain intact."

My tired head twirled in a merry-go-round-type fashion. "So that means we can't change anything?"

"No. It means we must attempt to make this moment come about another way."

We all waited for her to elaborate.

"You must still meet our king in the time you are born. You must still have a reason to come here. You must close the loop."

"What is she saying?" Teddi asked.

I looked at her, not even knowing where to begin. "She's saying we have a lot to figure out."

"As for the matter of Hagne," the woman went on, "we believe she should be sentenced to death. She has repeatedly violated our laws and we fear we cannot save her black heart from ruining us all."

"No," King barked out. "We will not allow this. We do not execute women and certainly not the woman who was betrothed to me from birth."

I hated to say it, but... "Killing her only makes conflict between the Seers and the regular people. Maybe you can send her away or something. Better yet, trade her with one of those nice fishermen from the mainland."

"No. She must die," the woman said. "Our ancestors say that she is the reason our people vanish and that this 10 Club Mia speaks of will never exist if we survive."

She could be right. Having more Seers in the world might have prevented all that, but who knew?

The woman approached King, and he took a small step back.

He fears her?

Couldn't blame him, really. Seers were a little scary. Especially these ones. The energy around them had the entire room buzzing and the hair on my arms standing straight up.

"But, my King, as is our tradition, Hagne's parents will not mourn for long. They will be compensated for their loss and given another daughter." She turned and looked at me and Teddi.

Uh-oh. One of us had to volunteer?

"Can I ask," I said, "at what point can we go back? We have family and friends and—"

"For the moment," she replied, "you cannot go anywhere. Not unless you wish for all of the events to remain intact as they were."

So we had to stay here? King would not be happy and it definitely pained me to be around him. All I saw was a man I loved. He saw me as vermin.

He caught me staring and snarled.

Yep, it's official. Our relationship had gone through the full spectrum. Hate. Love. Grief. Mistrust. Pain. Joy. We'd had it all. *And add…indifference. This ought to be interesting.*

But if this was the sacrifice required, the one I said I always knew I'd make for the people I loved, then I had to do it. 10 Club couldn't be defeated, so it had to be killed before it was ever born. Still, it pained me to think of never seeing my parents or friends again.

"So once we stay here and figure all this out, 10 Club will die." I wanted her confirmation, and she nodded. It was all I needed.

I wondered what else would change if I managed a miracle and stopped 10 Club from forming. Did that mean Justin, my brother, would live, too? Because no 10 Club meant Justin's path would never cross with any of them. I wanted to believe yes.

King rose to address the room. "This is all wonderful planning, but I am king, and I do not agree to this…" he waved his hand through the air, "this insanity. There will be no executions, no foreigners taking up residence here on our island and absolutely," he shot me a look, "no marriages."

"But, sir," the silver-haired woman argued, "you do not understand. We have spoken to our ancestors, the Seers who have passed, and—"

"How am I to know what they have told you or if they are real? I know two things—my home and my people. The gods decide the rest and they have not spoken to me. Get these two off my island." He turned to us, his gaze sizzling with anger. "And do not return. Not if you value your lives."

I glanced at Teddi, feeling too tired to give her any words of hope. "It's a no-go. He's kicking us out."

"What! Well…*fuck* him!" She rushed at King, screaming, "Fuck you! Do you have any fucking idea what I've been through? Do you!"

"Teddi, don't!" I charged after her. "You're not helping the situation."

"Silence!" King raised his hand to slap her, and I stepped in.

"Don't you dare," I growled. "Or so help me, I will remove your arm."

"You dare speak to me like that?"

"You think," I stepped closer, hugging Arch and tilting him away from King, "that I'm afraid of you?

You?" I laughed. "Buddy, you don't have a clue what I've been through—thanks to you, I might add. I've died and come back to life. I've watched the man I love—you!—live through hell and go mad. I've had my heart broken by you a million different ways, including you cheating on me with some crazy whore just so you could save Mack—I mean, Callias—for the fifteenth time. I watched my brother murdered. I watched myself turn into a murderer. I have been broken down and put back together so many fucking times that there's no part of my body or soul that's an original part!" I poked his chest. "So go ahead, King. Raise your hand to me. Call me a liar. Tell me you hate me or think I'm crazy. But I will *never*," I spat, "*never* fucking cower from you or anyone. Not again. Not ever." I took a breath, realizing I was doing no good. I was out of control. "You know what?" I stepped back. "Go ahead. Marry Hagne. Watch everything you love die. End up cursed for three thousand years. Be my fucking guest." I looked at Teddi. "Let's go home."

"We can't, Mia. They'll be there waiting for us." She placed her hand on her stomach.

I looked down at my feet. *We are not helpless. We don't have to accept this.*

I turned to the old woman. "How long will it take to train her?" I glanced at Teddi.

She blinked. "Years. It takes years, sometimes decades to show a Seer such as this the full range of her powers."

"We just need her ready to fight Hagne and the other assholes who are going to try to kill us when we go back."

"I can teach her what she needs to know in two weeks."

I nodded. "Good. And what will it take to get my powers back?"

She looked shocked. "I do not know. We will need to consult with the ancestors who struck the bargain with you."

"Okay. Let them know I gave up my powers to be with King." I looked him up and down. "But I don't need him anymore. I just need to fight 10 Club."

King glared at me with purified, concentrated hate.

"Don't give me that look, Draco Minos. You are *not* my king. You do *not* get to look at me like that."

I walked from the room with Teddi on my tail.

"Mia, what just happened?"

"We're on our own. That's what happened."

CHAPTER SEVENTEEN

King did not follow through with his threat to kick us off the island like some *Survivor, Time Warp Edition* rejects. However, he did not come and see us or lift a finger to help. Arch began a diet of boiled barley and goat milk. I also gave him the little breast milk I carried and boiled water with mashed grapes that I filtered with linen. I did everything I could to keep him fed, clean, and safe. Meanwhile, Teddi and I, both pregnant and feeling sicker than hell, ate bread, lentils, boiled water and grape juice, too. Our bodies were not used to whatever microbes they had in this time and we both needed to train, not sit on a toilet. Or squat over a pit. Whichever.

Teddi stayed with the elderly Seer woman, who we learned was named Ptolema, which meant "warlike." *Love it. Exactly what we need.* A Seer who could fight. Everyone called her Lema or Aunt Lema, however. She was the matriarch of the island. Anyway, Lema decided to have Teddi focus on very specific gifts such as learning how to channel her powers to misdirect, make others feel fear for no apparent reason, and to see a face that wasn't hers. Not easy for Teddi, who was the kind of Seer born with the extraordinary gift of healing. Funnily enough, her profession, prior to learning about her very unique past, was a psychologist. The first time I'd met her was at a clinic in Santa Barbara, where she'd been trying to treat a suicidal man who suffered from "delusions" of being cursed and the twin brother of the ancient king of Minoa. Joke was on her.

Anyway, Lema knew what the future-Hagne was capable of because she'd been training her for years. This allowed Teddi to focus on skills that would give us a higher probability of getting out of that 10 Club party alive.

As for me, I had no powers, so I could only help in other ways. Hand to hand. Or in 1400 BC, that meant sword fighting.

"So I do like this?" I asked, lunging with a long dagger toward the olive tree trunk while the guard—yes, a Spiros who seemed inexplicably devoted to me—tirelessly tried to teach me the moves.

"Yes. Plant your left foot firmly into the earth and lunge with your right hand. When your opponent shifts to your left, you keep your footing. Like this." He showed me the dance, pretending to stab the bundle of reeds wrapped around the tree. From the scars on the bark, I guessed this was their state-of-the-art mortal combat training center.

"Here goes." I clumsily followed his moves.

"No, no. Your weight is on the wrong foot." He proceeded to correct me by jerking my shoulders from behind. Every stroke and move was a counter of sorts to keep the tip of the opponent's blade away. You waited until the other person made a wrong dance move, giving you a clean shot at a vital organ.

This is incredibly stupid. 10 Club members don't duel with swords. All I really needed was to get my hands on a gun while Teddi took care of Hagne. Then we'd run like hell and hope to find some other way to end 10 Club. King had to have something else in that warehouse of his. We simply needed to get inside and not die.

"You are not holding your sword correctly," said King from a wide stone bench on the other side of the enclosed courtyard, where Arch slept in a basket, wrapped in a blanket. How long had King been sitting there?

I looked away, ignoring how casually he sat next to his infant son, treating him like a stranger. How could King not know his own flesh and blood?

I ignored him and went back to whacking the bundle of reeds tied to the tree.

"Leave us," King said to his guard before standing and strutting over like a giant peacock flashing his giant feathers. Only, King had his impressive muscular build, six-three height, and stunning blue eyes in lieu of feathers.

He frowned at me with those feathers. "I have never seen such a poor student." He turned and looked at the guard, whose feet seemed stuck to the dirt. "Why are you still here?"

"No. Stay," I said to the guard. "The king has better things to do with his time."

"The king gave you an order. Now leave." King put his hand on the hilt of his sword at his side.

The man gave me a conflicted look.

"Do not look at her," said King. "You answer to me."

"Uh...actually, no," I cut in. "You made all of the Spiros loyal to me. You used some sort of spell."

King frowned. "You lie."

"Do I?" I looked at the guard. "Punch him. Punch your king."

The man raised his fist, and King caught it.

The look on King's face—tomato red, with a death stare in his blue eyes—was priceless.

"Okay. Thank you," I said, taking pity on the poor man, "you can go."

He dipped his head and scurried off.

"Nice trick, you witch," King growled.

I knew that "witch" was not the real word he used, but that was how the tattoo on my wrist translated it. What King likely meant was that I wasn't a good Seer. He believed I used my abilities for personal gain—greed and power. Evil.

"Whatever," I said. "I'm done trying to win you over." I turned and went back to my practice, imagining Hagne coming at me in the room where Teddi and I had been hiding out. In my head it all seemed so simple: Take out Hagne. Run outside and keep running until we found a way to kill them. However, reality was far different. A million things could go wrong.

"So you truly mean to go back to this place you came from," King said.

"Yes," I panted.

"Fighting with a child strapped to your back," he said, his voice full of judgment.

"And one in the oven," I snapped. "Not like you left me with a whole hell of a lot of choices."

"You could stay here."

"Here?" I didn't look at him.

"Not on this island, of course. I meant you could stay in this time, though I do not believe you are truly from another era. This is impossible."

I huffed. "Stay here? Running around on the mainland in a time where unmarried women without family are made into slaves or raped and murdered? No, thank you. I'll take my chances."

I stepped forward and poked a little spot in the reeds that I imagined was Hagne's heart.

"Woman, you do not stand a chance against a turnip. You hold the sword as if it were a wet fish you do not wish to touch."

They had turnips in this time? I had to get me some. My pregnancy cravings were really kicking in and I absolutely loved those dim sum turnip patties.

My mouth began to salivate. "I don't need to win a sword fight. I just need to run from a blood-bath. If I'm lucky, I'll get a hold of a gun."

"What is a gun?"

"It's a weapon. You hold it, and it shoots pieces of metal at very fast speeds. You know what?" I turned to face him, dropping the heavy long dagger to my side. "Why are you even here other than to distract me?" Being near him, seeing him like this—alive, breathing, shirtless and untainted by every-thing that was to come—wasn't easy. Because this man was who I fell in love with. He loved his people. He worked hard to protect them. He was a good, good man with a strong but big heart. And, of course, there was that body covered only by a piece of red cloth around his waist, showing off his deep olive skin, bulging biceps, and chiseled pecs and abs. Whatever workout routine he had, the man looked powerful and sexier than sin. And those eyes... *Breathtaking.* Intense, acutely aware, and deep blue mixed with hints of turquoise green like the beauti-ful ocean around the island. His long black hair, which fell loose around his shoulders, only made his eyes look bluer.

He made a grumble deep in his chest. "Turn around."

"Why?"

"Must you always be so combative? Just turn, woman."

I glared at him, but begrudgingly did as he

asked.

"Good, now stand like this and hold the sword like that." Pressing his warm hard body against my back, he kicked my legs apart and grabbed my hands, pushing the sword in my right hand out in front of me. The heat of him on my back, the feel of his cock against my ass, instantly made my blood flow faster. My body remembered him like it remembered the need to breathe. King had been the type of man who showed no mercy in the bedroom. He took control, he fucked hard, and he knew his way around a woman's body. He always left me begging for more.

My body igniting, I stepped forward, putting some air between us. "Thanks. Got it." I glanced at him over my shoulder.

He simply stood there with an intense, angry gaze. "I am merely trying to help you."

"Help me?" I tilted my head. "You are trying to *help* me." I laughed. That was hysterical.

"What is it that you find so humorous, woman?"

"Nothing." I shook my head at my bare feet. I hadn't come here with shoes, and since I'd been demoted to unwelcome invader from another land, they hadn't offered to make me any. In any case, his refusal to accept who I was made it impossible to find a solution—a way to change events. We were stuck with going back and fighting 10 Club on our own. "Yeah. Thank you for 'the help.'"

He crossed his meaty arms over his bare chest. "I could've had you thrown into the ocean."

"A pregnant woman?" I didn't believe a word of it. "You don't have it in you, King. And you can stop the tough-guy act. I know you."

"Do you now?"

"Better than I know myself."

"And tell me." He bent down, shoving his face into mine. His breath was minty and made me want to kiss him for a taste. Did he have any clue how being near him like this pained me. It was a complete mind fuck to love him as much as I did and for him not to know me at all. "What is it you think you know?"

I gazed into his sapphire blue eyes and sighed. "Your belief in being good and your loyalty to the people you love are everything to you. You'd rather die than betray them. You're also a fighter. You refuse to give up."

"I think you speak in general terms that could apply to almost any man."

I shrugged. "I suppose. But I've never met anyone who refused to die or stay dead. Your stubbornness transcends the boundaries of space and time."

"Ah. You are referring to your little story about my cursed spirit walking the earth for thousands of years in search of you."

His glib tone didn't sit well with me. "I don't need this, King. I get it. You don't believe me. And you don't have to. History will find a way to play out."

He laughed. "Only, you claim I fall in love with you, something which is clearly impossible."

I couldn't lie. His words stung. "That's because you killed the version of me you fell in love with. You broke her. Now, if you don't mind, this smarter, more serious version of myself has to figure out how to survive against the most powerful and demented bastards on the planet that *you* created. Thanks for that, by the way."

His eyes twitched with irritation. If I had to guess, I'd say he was debating throttling me or throwing me into that sinking boat again.

"Brother, there you are." A spitting image of King, wearing a dark blue cloth around his waist and his hair pulled back into a braid, walked into the courtyard. "I came as soon as I received the message from Lema. What has happened?"

"Mack," I whispered. I couldn't help but stare. He looked so young and bright. He hadn't been tortured and killed and broken by 10 Club. He was still just the king's playboy brother, who lived a carefree life.

"She should not have summoned you. This is no concern of yours," King said.

"Like hell it isn't," I grumbled.

"Silence, or I will have your tongue removed," King barked at me.

I laughed. "Yeah, right. You're too nice for

that."

"Who is she?" Mack asked, only he went by his first name in this era. Callias. Callias Macarias Minos. Mack was short for Macarias.

"Hi. I'm your sister-in-law, Mia. And your pregnant, grieving widow is with Lema. You should really go meet her."

Mack's dark brows knitted together in confusion.

King shook his head. "Do not pay her any attention. She is mad. And she is leaving."

"I'm not mad. You're stubborn. And your brother deserves to hear the truth and make up his own mind. This affects him, too."

"No one asked you, Seer," King barked. "Now leave, or I'll have the guards carry you out." His eyes locked with mine but then dropped down to my breasts for a moment and then to my lips. *Yep. He's still King.* Feistiness still rang his bell.

"Callias," I said, looking at King, "your brother is a giant horse's ass."

"What's a horse?" Mack asked.

"Never mind." I walked over to retrieve Arch. He'd be awake soon and would want to eat, so I had to go prepare our food in the kitchen—really a room with a few pots, utensils, and a fire. King's house slaves let us cook in there since they were afraid of us and Lema warned everyone to be kind. The Seers carried a lot of weight around here.

As I picked up Arch, I heard Mack and King

beginning to bicker. Mack insisted King explain why a strange woman with golden hair was on their island, and King tried to brush him off. Then the two started really going at it.

I hoped Mack didn't back down. At the very least, he had to meet Teddi. Maybe he would believe our story and persuade King to try to find a new path forward. For them, for us, for their people.

CHAPTER EIGHTEEN

I spent the rest of the afternoon with Arch while Teddi stayed with Lema, who gave her a coveted spit tat and taught her how to be a Seer that could do more than simply heal. The slaves in the kitchen were already worried about what they'd heard: Their people would go to war and disappear if King didn't listen to me. They also asked about Teddi. Was it true she could heal? When I'd replied yes, they gasped. "She must be a favorite of the gods. Why is our king shunning her? We will be punished."

Ha. Take that, King. Your people think you're a bonehead for being mean to us.

Teddi ran into our room, where I sat on a crudely made burlap blanket, playing peekaboo with Arch. "Mia! Ohmygod. I met him. I met him!"

"Who?" From her excitement I would've guessed Elvis, something not so entirely impossible given all of the craziness we were encountering.

"Mack! Oh god. He's so…different. But he's still him. He recognized me right away."

I stood up and propped Arch onto my hip. "He

remembers you?"

"He couldn't take his eyes off me and just kept saying, 'I know you. I know you.' It completely freaked him the hell out, and he ran away. Maybe it's our connection and my Seer gift—they're somehow helping him see what I see." Her wide green eyes teared up.

"Are you okay?" I put my free hand on her arm.

"Yes." She scrubbed her face with her hands. "No. I miss him, Mia. I miss him so much, and seeing him just now…" She dropped her arms and shook her head rapidly, blowing out a breath to shake it off. "I'm okay. I just didn't realize how much I'd bottled up since he died." She looked at me. "I feel like this was supposed to happen, Mia. I was supposed to come here and find him again and get the chance to do it all over. No curses. No 10 Club. Just…us."

"So you want to stay here?" I asked Teddi.

"Lema told me if I do, it could help change the course for the Minoans. I'm a new element to the equation."

"What about Hagne? She's in love with Mack and engaged to King. She'll come after you one way or another."

Teddi shook her head. "The elders already decided to disobey King. They will kill her and I will be offered as a replacement to her family."

"You really think that's going to work? People are not interchangeable."

"They're Seers. They don't think like we do. They answer to a higher power, and to them, it's all about balancing out the elements that rule their world. And they talk to their dead ancestors on a regular basis, which is very disturbing. Especially as a psychologist."

"I still don't understand how this all works out. I mean, if Mack never gets caught up in the Hagne drama, then he never goes to Mexico to meet you."

Teddi slowly moved her head from side to side. "Lema says if I stay, the events will realign somehow. It has to, because I'm here, aren't I?"

Ah, the old "fate doesn't like contradictions" argument that Lema had made to King.

"What about your parents?" They were alive and retired in Arizona somewhere.

"I think that my parents would want me to be happy. That's all they ever wanted."

I looked into her big green eyes. She looked so damned happy, and I didn't want to rob her of that, but things were not so simple. "I know you want to be with Mack, but King won't let me stay and I can't fight 10 Club alone."

"I know," she said triumphantly, "and that's why you're going to go back with King."

I nearly choked on my tongue. "Sorry?"

"You, Arch, King. You all return."

Another King substitute-impersonator plan? "It would never work, and even it if could, King would never leave his people. Never."

"What if he doesn't have the choice?"

"You mean kidnap him? Oh. That would be an excellent choice. I could listen to him yell at me for the next fifty years until I grow old and die."

"I'm not kidding, Mia. Think about how that would change things."

"If he left, who will rule here?"

"Mack. I'll help him. The Seers will help him. There will be no brotherly duel. No war. And the Seers will live."

"It's too risky, Teddi. We have absolutely no idea what I'll be facing when I get back." Then there was the issue of not having King's cooperation. He'd be pissed. And in shock.

She grabbed my shoulder. "No. You're missing the point. If King stays here without a commitment to change things, then history will likely repeat. Maybe the war will start because the Seers kill Hagne without King's approval. Or maybe King gets into a conflict some other way and still ends up cursed. We don't know. But if you take him with you, and I stay here to live out my days and help these people, we could avoid every horrible thing that ever happened. King won't become cursed. The 10 Club won't ever be created. It all goes away."

Oh. I hadn't thought of that. It did make sense; however, we were trying to outguess and outsmart a million different events that had all led us to this exact moment. "Honestly, I feel like we're trapped in an impossible, dizzying maze of variables my brain can't come close to comprehending." Arch started pulling on a lock of my hair. I unwrapped his chubby little fingers and switched him to the other hip.

"Mia, what I'm talking about is bigger than trying to influence the variables. Think of it as if we're playing chess on a giant board, only we're going to remove the board altogether."

The fact that she believed in this plan so concretely gave me reason to question my doubts, but at the end of the day, we were all still guessing.

"I need to think, Teddi. It's…a lot. A lot-a lot."

"A lot. Got it."

"What have you done to my brother?" growled a deep voice from the open doorway. We both turned to find King standing there, fists balled, face rage red, lungs pumping. His gaze was locked onto Teddi.

I instinctively stepped between them. "Calm down, King. She didn't do—"

"Silence!" he yelled. "This has gone far enough." He looked over his shoulder. "Put them in cages."

Several men in red skirts rushed into the room.

"You can't do this to us," I said.

"You think you can come to my home and try to take over? You think you and the Seers can do as you please? Disobey me? Put spells on my brother? You do not know me." His nostrils flared. "You do not know how far I will go to protect my people from the likes of you. Take them."

CHAPTER NINETEEN

Fearing that Arch might get hurt, I didn't fight the guards, who were apparently not Spiros because they did not seem to give a flying Minoan fuck about putting two pregnant women and a baby into cages. At least, I'd hoped that was where Teddi went, because they'd separated us.

But as I sat there in a crudely built cage made of branches and barely tall enough for me to stand, my mind quickly plummeted into a fit of panic. *Shit, shit, shit, it's starting all over again.*

The moment the Seers found out that King had jailed us, they would come to our aid. The people had already begun to see Teddi as a gift from the gods with her healing powers. And if Mack truly felt a connection with Teddi, he might not be so happy about this outcome either. I could see a million different ways this situation would end in tragedy, King dead and cursed.

My skin began to crawl, remembering how sadistic and cruel King had become when he'd been cursed. Even he called himself a monster during his more lucid moments.

No. No. This can't be our fate.

I knew I would have to do what Teddi asked and try to steal King. I would have to take a bold leap and pray it was the right choice.

"Hey!" I called out to the guards on the other side of the fenced-in area that looked like a twisted people zoo, with several rows of cages. Thankfully, it was winter, so we weren't cooking as the sun hit high noon. "Hey!" I called out. "Tell the king I need to talk to him. Tell him I'm ready to leave."

The guards didn't pay me any attention.

"Look," I said. "I understand you probably sit here all day, listening to people beg and complain. But you and I both know the Seers are not going to let this go unpunished. Fighting will break out. People will die. And I'm sure you don't want that."

The guards didn't even blink in my general direction.

I continued, "I'm not asking you to free me. I'm just asking you to tell the king that I want to speak to him, that I'm willing to leave. Today. I just need to see him first. Please."

One of the men gave a slight nod and waved over another guard. "Stand post. I will go see our king." He walked away calmly, but as the hours passed, I realized he wasn't coming back.

Fuck. This just kept getting worse and worse.

∽ ∾

About three or four hours later—didn't have a watch, so who knew for sure?—another man with light brown hair and scars on his chest came to let me out. From his size and temperament, I had the impression that this man was a warrior.

King thinks I'm dangerous. Wonderful. How would I get close to him now?

The man let me and Arch out of our crude jail cell and led us out of the fenced-in area and through a tall set of wooden gates outside the king's compound.

"Where are we going?" I said, bouncing a now screaming wet baby, following along a dirt road filled with sharp rocks.

Dammit. I miss shoes.

"Lema's home. You are expected there." He pointed toward a small cluster of whitewashed houses with a pen filled with goats to one side. "It is the one to the far right."

"Thanks." I gave him a quick nod and carefully walked to the small dwelling. "Hello?" I peeked my head inside the two-room cottage with plaster-covered walls and hearth. No windows or door.

"Mia!" Teddi sat at a small table in the corner with Lema. Her eyes looked all puffy and red.

"Miss me?" I said.

"Oh God." She rushed over and gave me a hug. "Are you two alright?"

"He put me in a cage. It was lovely. And you?"

"Same. But I wasn't there long. Mack got me

out." She looked at Arch, who kept crying. "Oh, you poor thing. Did your evil daddy lock you up?" she said in a pouty tone. "Here. Let me change him. I've got some boiled milk and barley already started."

Arch stopped crying the moment she touched him. Soothing Seer powers. *They need to bottle that stuff.*

"Thank you." I sighed exasperatedly.

She smiled and took him into the other room.

"So what happened?" I asked Lema, who sat at her little table, sipping from a clay cup.

"Please, sit. Can I offer you some wine?"

"Normally I'd say yes, but I'm pregnant and have a feeling I'm going to need a clear head to deal with whatever is happening." The air around us buzzed with tension, and it was not coming from me.

"There has been much debate and negotiation with our king. A deal was struck. The Seers promised not to harm Hagne if he released the two of you."

I really hadn't wanted Hagne killed, despite her black heart, but that was only because her death seemed to be a catalyst for so many events. Other than that reason, however, she didn't deserve to breathe. Not after everything she'd done to me.

"Okay. So no war?" I asked.

"No."

This was good. This was great! Except…Hagne

would still be a threat to King and Mack. *Dammit. Dammit.* We were going down the same path. I could feel it in my heart. I could taste the doom in the air.

"And what about Hagne? She'll try to hurt Teddi and Mack."

"Teddi has agreed to cure Hagne. She will remove whatever sickness is in her soul, but as Teddi is now learning, there is always a cost when a Seer uses her gifts."

"So it could be dangerous?"

Teddi came into the room, holding a happy, laughing little Arch. His bright blue eyes and happy pink lips melted my heart.

"Are you going to cure Hagne?" I asked Teddi.

"I'm going to try, but I'll wait until after the baby is born. In the meantime, we'll have to keep an eye on her."

I nodded, trying to think it through. "So you still want to stay?"

She took my hand. "It's okay, Mia. I spoke to Mack—I mean, Callias—he understands what's happening. And I have faith in us. Especially since seeing each other here feels like the first time." For them, it had been love at first sight, their connection deep and unbreakable. "I love him, Mia. Just like I always have."

"But you know he's not exactly the same man. Things will be different."

"It doesn't matter. I can't leave Callias."

"Did someone say my name?" Mack stood in the doorway with a slight twinkle in his eyes, which were stuck to Teddi.

Teddi's face lit up. She was so in love with him, and it made me jealous. I hated the mishmash of feelings inside me that coated the love in my heart like a dirty blanket.

"Hi, Callias," I said. "Thank you for helping us."

He dipped his head. "A man knows when fate is calling, and if he doesn't, he doesn't deserve to live." He winked at Teddi, who sat with Arch, feeding him a little milk mush. He was too hungry to squabble.

Callias walked over to her and kneeled in front of Arch, watching him with a sort of loving fascination. After several long moments, he sighed. "This will not be easy for me, losing my brother. But there is nothing I wouldn't do for him or for our people."

"So you told him?" I asked Teddi, referring to the plan to bring King home with me.

"I needed him to put his faith in me, so I put my faith in him first." She beamed at him.

That had been a risky move, but it was helpful to have Mack on board.

"So you see, Mia," said Lema, "the pieces are falling into place. Now you must go to the king. It is time for you to leave before fate molds the events in a nonreversible direction, as they once were."

Fate was already hard at work. I could feel

something bad, something horrible floating in the air, waiting to strike.

"And, Mia," she added, "the ancestors say that your gifts will never be returned. A deal was struck to create balance. It cannot be undone."

I stared down at my dirty, sore feet. "I figured that."

Lema got up and walked over, laying her hand on my arm. "They also say you must leave this place immediately and never return. You or the child inside you. It would only create more risk."

I hadn't planned on returning, but God only knew what would happen when I went back. The possibilities were endless. I would also miss Teddi with all my heart. She felt like more than a friend. She was like a sister.

"Christ." I drew a deep breath and then looked at Callias, who stood and took hold of a messy, but happy little Arch. "Please, promise you'll take good care of Teddi."

"I will do my best." He bowed his head of long black hair.

I looked at Teddi. "And please be careful. Hagne is dangerous."

"We will make sure she's no longer a threat once we find her," Callias replied.

"What do you mean, find her?" I asked.

"She has run away," Callias said.

"Oh, great." Psycho-Seer was on the loose.

"It's okay, Mia," said Teddi. "She can't get far.

We're on an island."

"Let us handle Hagne. It is time for you to go." Lema scooched me out the door. "Hurry now."

"Okay, okay. I'm going." I grabbed Arch, who watched the drama with wide blue eyes, from Callias. I then looked at Teddi. I couldn't bear to say goodbye. Especially like this. I would never see her again.

She hugged me and Arch. "Take care, Mia. I promise to write every day." She pulled away and smiled. "You'll feel like you were right here with us."

My eyes teared. She'd be long dead the moment I got back home. *Wait.* I glanced at her hand. "You're still wearing the ring."

It used to be King's, but he gave it to her right before he'd saved Mack. King told her to take good care of his brother, and the ring would keep her from aging and dying as long as she wore it. He'd made one for Arch and me, too. I had taken mine off after King left us. I couldn't stand the thought of living forever without the man I loved. Arch's ring was in the safe with mine. King had thought to give it to him when he was grown.

Teddi glanced at her finger with the shiny little diamond embedded securely in a gold band. "I...I don't think I'll keep it on, Mia. I don't want to watch everyone else get old." Meaning, she didn't want to live forever. Not if that meant leaving everyone else behind.

"I understand." I squeezed her hand, feeling my heart tear just a little more. Everything was happening so fast, and little by little, I was losing everyone. "Have a wonderful life, Teddi. And give that baby a big kiss for me when she comes. Okay?"

"I will." She gave me a hug, and I couldn't let go.

"My brother will be in his chambers," said Callias, urging us apart. "Come this way, Mia." He gave a longing glance at Teddi. Yes, those two were already goo-goo ape shit over each other. "I will return shortly," Callias said with a cocky little smile and began walking.

I took one last look at Teddi, committing her face to memory. "Good luck." Holding Arch tightly in my arms, I followed him back the way we came, up the dirt road to the tall wooden gates that led to the outer perimeter of the king's compound. The two sword-toting guards let us pass immediately.

"What's King going to do when he sees me here?" I asked.

"Let me handle him. You focus on making things right for my nephew." Callias flashed a smile over his broad shoulders. I loved his confidence, but it wasn't enough to calm my nervous stomach.

We passed through a small fig orchard and reached the building overlooking the ocean. It had big pillars in front and elaborate patterns in blue and red paint on the outside. Suddenly, memories of being here with King during my first trip hit hard. The way he'd made love to me—ravenous and passionate. The long soaks in his tub. Talking for hours about his parents and how he felt growing up, knowing he'd be responsible for so many people. The time we spent here had been short but cemented this man in my heart. Funny how he couldn't stand the sight of me now.

Just wait until you kidnap him. He's going to hate you on a whole new level. My heart and stomach knotted with sadness. God, my feelings were so messed up. I had been through so much with King—the deepest love, the most crushing heartbreak—I didn't know which way was up, but I knew I loved him. I always would. Still, given the way things had turned out, I had to wonder if we were simply never meant to be. *I mean, look how Teddi and Callias turned out.* The events had done nothing to dull their passion.

Besides, it doesn't matter if King doesn't love you anymore. You still have to do this, Mia. I lifted my chin. I had to be fast and just take him. *Band-Aid. Rip.*

"Brother!" Mack called out as we approached the doorway guarded by two more men. It seemed there was an endless supply of soldiers on the island. "I have brought someone to see you."

King emerged looking pissier than ever—dark brows pulled together into angry ridges, nostrils slightly flared, lips mashed together, and jaw tighter than a pair of bolt cutters. The moment he saw me, he exploded. "You dare bring this witch to my doorstep?" King yelled.

Mack held out his hands. "Listen to me. We don't have much time."

"Time for what?" King spat.

Callias looked at me. This was my cue. I began to focus my energy on the tiny little life inside my belly, but she was quiet, possibly sleeping.

Dammit, sweetie. Wake up. Wake up. But did I really need that? Her blood and power ran through my body. I knew because King had used it to resurrect his evil posse.

Okay. Just focus. How did I trigger it last time? I'd been in a state of high emotion. Death and fear. *Jesus.* Did my life always have to be in danger in order for a miracle to happen?

"What is she doing?" King snapped.

"Mia?" Callias urged. "Do you have something *important* to say to my brother?"

My gaze toggled between both men. "Yes. It's just…I need a moment to gather my thoughts." I closed my eyes. *Come on, little one. Give Mommy some Seer juice. Help Mommy take Daddy home with us.*

Nothing happened, even though I could feel her little warm light glowing inside me.

Maybe I needed to retreat and see if Lema knew what to do? What other option was there? I couldn't stand here all day. Not when King was damned ready to toss me out of his compound on my ass.

Okay, just tell him you're here to say you're very sorry for everything you've done. I didn't want him to become suspicious that I was up to something and throw me in the twig stockade again.

"King, I just want to say—" I opened my eyes just as a female figure with long brown hair came charging around the corner behind King, with a dagger posed to strike.

Hagne!

Still holding Arch, I instinctively pushed King to the side and twisted my body to shield Arch. I felt the knife slice along my shoulder blade and into my back.

I screamed but managed to stay on my feet, unwilling to let go of Arch or risk falling on him.

Callias jumped on Hagne and began wrestling the blade away. Meanwhile, King got his footing straight. The look in his eyes as he met my gaze, only for a second, was sheer confusion.

King quickly grabbed Arch from my arms as I fell over.

As I lay there, I heard the faint sounds of Hagne grunting and then a crunching noise mixed into Arch's cries.

"Go quickly! Bring that Teddi woman now," King called out right before I lost consciousness.

CHAPTER TWENTY

Well, goddammit. How many times did a girl have to die before she deserved a little happiness? I mean, hell. What was this, number three?

The first time, I'd been wearing that special ring King made for me. It was awful because the ring didn't actually prevent death. I still had to go through the pain of dying. The ring then sort of woke me back up. *Terrifying.* The second time I'd died, I'd made a deal with the Seers to give up my powers if they allowed me to come back. This time? Ugh. I had nothing to bargain with.

"Fuck you, death. You suck," I muttered to myself.

"Ah, but I am not death," I heard King's deep hypnotic voice, "and you are not dead."

The pain in my body became sharper as my brain clicked back on. "Ariadna?" I gasped. "Is she alright?"

King's bloodshot blue eyes greeted me. "Lema says you will both be fine, though you will be weak for several days and have lost a lot of blood." He sat on the edge of the padded stone bed right next to me.

I drew a painful breath. My lungs didn't feel right, my arms didn't feel right, and my back felt raw.

"What happened?" I mumbled weakly.

"Before or after Hagne tried to kill me?"

"After," I whispered.

"Callias broke her neck, and your Seer companion closed the wound. I must admit, I have never seen anything like it."

Just wait until you see your time-traveling fetus.

Speaking of babies, "Where's Arch?"

"He is right here." King jerked his head to the basket next to him. "He's been changed, fed, and is sleeping now."

"Is he okay?" I muttered.

"Yes. It took a while to rock him to sleep—he is a little fighter, that one."

"I'll have to thank Teddi. When is she coming back?" I whispered.

"What makes you believe that I am incapable of rocking a child?" King crossed his thick biceps over his bare chest.

"You rocked him?"

King stood with a straight back. "I am a man of many talents." He grinned proudly.

"Thank you."

"I am the one who is grateful." He scratched his short black beard. "But might I ask why you risked your life and that of your child to save me?"

I made a little hissing sound. It felt too embarrassing to tell him how much I loved him. "It was instinctual."

"No. Mothers instinctually move to protect their children. You put yourself into harm's way. For me."

"I didn't feel like Arch was in danger—I mean, I felt like...I could...Okay, it was stupid. I really wasn't thinking." I drew a slow, pain-filled breath.

King pulled up a small wooden stool next to the basket holding Arch, and sat, bobbing his head of thick black hair. "So you instinctually want to protect me," he said quietly as if thinking out loud.

"Something like that," I whispered.

He nodded and then looked down at his hands, which were resting on his lap across his little man skirt, his large slightly hairy thighs exposed.

He drew a breath. "I have to say, Mia, that your actions have given me reason to doubt my assumptions about you. A woman would never take such a risk unless she truly loved a man."

I looked away, my heart and body too tender to cope with this conversation.

"You do love me," he said. "More than your own life and as much as you love that child."

Well, the way I loved Arch and Ariadna were very different from the way I loved King, but I supposed if it could be measured, they'd come pretty close. Without a doubt, I would give my life for any one of them.

"Don't let it go to your head," I said.

He leaned forward, planting his elbows on his thighs. "I do not understand what that means. But you truly are my wife, aren't you?"

"Yes," I replied quietly.

"And he is truly mine?" He glanced down at Arch.

"Yes."

He nodded slowly as if trying to soak it all in. "And I died before you came here?"

"To save Callias. You gave him your body so that he could live and be with Teddi. But then you returned. You, but not you."

"I see." His brows furrowed and lips tightened. "Mia, I would like you to tell me everything. From the beginning. As much detail as you can provide."

"Why?" I blinked at him.

"I believe the Seers were right; fate wishes us to be together." He placed his warm strong hand over mine. "And I cannot deny that I have waited my entire life to find a woman as brave as you."

"So you don't hate me anymore?"

"You are quite lovely to look at, so that does help matters." He grinned and it was his trademark charming smile.

My heart got all fluttery. *There's my King.*

"I am sorry for the way I treated you," he added. "I promise it will never happen again."

I could hardly believe this change in him. It

made me want to weep with joy and jump up and down. I loved him so deeply and this made me want to believe, foolish as it might be, in us. That we might find a path forward again.

I chuckled softly, trying not to provoke my wound. "If I'd known it would just take getting stabbed by Hagne to get you to believe me, I would've started out with that."

His warm smile melted away. "Seeing you lying on the ground, bleeding, is something I never wish to repeat."

"Me neither."

"Then let us proceed. Tell me how we came to meet. Tell me our story."

I swallowed the lump in my throat. "It all started when my brother went missing in Mexico. You were the only person willing to help me. For a price…"

∽ ∾

It took several hours to tell King our story again, this time with more detail—about how we met, how he'd become cursed and how history repeated after I came here the first time. He paced and listened. I breathed and tried to ignore my pain. When Arch woke, King called one of the servant girls to change him and feed him in the next room.

"So it seems," he said, "that Hagne initiated the events."

"Yes." I shifted on the bed—a stone platform covered in soft fabric stuffed with something cushy. King's bed was much nicer than what we'd been sleeping on. "But really, it's what happens after you die that starts all of this."

"I see now why you wish things to change, but I do not understand why you still love me. After all that I did, I would think you'd be happy to be rid of me."

An awkward silence filled the air.

"I guess I'm a sucker for three-thousand-year-old kings." I grinned weakly. "God, my back hurts like hell. Where is Teddi?"

"I told my men that no one is to disturb us. This is important, and I do not want to be interrupted. Please go on with the story. What happened after you returned from here the first time?"

Something didn't feel right. King's voice had a hint of worry.

"Is everything all right?" I asked.

He smiled down at me. "You have nothing to worry about, Mia. Please continue."

Weaker than hell, I completed the story. King and I getting married, having Arch, and Mack dying. Then there was the awesome part about 10 Club and King's super-fun buddies coming back to life in the name of world domination.

After I finished, King sat for a long time, scratching the back of his head, getting up and pacing the room, sitting again, and then pacing some more. I got the impression he wanted to say something, but didn't know how.

"What is it?"

Finally, he turned and looked at me with a hardness in his eyes. "Hagne is dead now; however the Seers wished to execute her. They will not be upset that Callias killed her, so there should be no war."

"I hope not, but things could change and repeat some other way. That's why I wanted to take you home. You can't become cursed, live three thousand years in pain, and create 10 Club if you come back with me. It changes the game completely."

He shook his head. "Come back with you?"

"Yes."

"You mean leave my people?"

I winced, trying to sit up. I knew that Teddi had closed any wounds, but I wasn't feeling any better. "The way to think about it isn't that you're leaving them, but saving them. It closes the door on a war with the Seers." It also eliminated his death—for now, at least—and becoming cursed and creating his evil empire.

"What if it is someone else who starts a war?" he asked.

"I don't know. Maybe it's your people's destiny to disappear. Maybe it's not. But what happens to you and the evil you facilitate is a thousand times worse, King. The 10 Club kill, rape, torture and do anything they like to anyone they like."

"Evil will always exist."

"Not like this."

"Mia! Ohmygod. Are you okay?" Teddi dashed into the room, her beige linen tunic dirty and soaked with sweat.

"I'm fine," I mumbled. "What happened to you?"

"Good." She turned to King and gave him a push. "What the hell, buddy! I had to jump over a wall to get in here and then your thugs chased me down."

"This is because I did not want to be disturbed," he snarled at her.

"Teddi, I'm okay," I warned, not wanting the two to go at it.

"No. It's not! You came this close to dying." She pinched an inch of air.

"Well, I'm okay now." Weak and in pain, but okay.

"Mia, that was way beyond a broken wrist or stomachache. I didn't have enough in me to fully heal you. Let me check you."

Before I could say anything, she had her hands on me.

"What are you doing?" I asked.

"Lema has been showing me how to read a person's light. Now be quiet. Let me concentrate." Teddi closed her eyes. "See. There. I feel it. You're still bleeding inside."

Shit. "That explains why it hurts to breathe so

much."

"You need to get to a hospital, Mia. I'm a healer, not a surgeon. My gift works better on emotions and psychological conditions."

"I already tried to go home, but I couldn't get it to work."

Teddi scratched the back of her head. "Okay. I'll go get Lema." She pointed at King. "And you! You better let me in this time or so help me—"

"May we cease with the threats for today?" he snapped. "I have had quite enough of them, especially from Seers."

Teddi shot poison darts with her green eyes. "Asshole." She turned and hightailed it out of there.

King looked down at me. "What is an asshole?"

"Never mind. She's not happy with you. That's all."

"And this place she says you must go? A hospital?"

"It's where they heal the sick, but the healers use medicines. Sometimes they use machines."

"Machines?"

"Those are—" A sharp pain exploded in my chest, and I felt hot lead pouring into my left lung. I wondered if that knife had punctured something. If so, Teddi was right. If she couldn't heal me, I needed a doctor.

"Mia?" King kneeled down beside me and stroked my forehead. "What is happening?"

"The pain," I ground out my words. "Oh God."

"You are not going to die on me, Mia. You cannot. I will not allow it."

How sweet that he thought he could order me not to die. "I don't know…" I rolled to my side, crying out in agony. All I could think about was poor little Ariadna.

"Hell." He got up and called to the guards. "Find out where those Seers are. Tell them to hurry!" He quickly returned to my side. "Tell me, Mia. Tell me why I waited so long to see you for who you really are? Cursed gods."

I loved his BC swearing. It was truly adorable. But at this moment, my heart was pounding in my chest and my vision turned all spotty.

"It's the story," I groaned, "of our lives. Tragedy."

"No. Do not speak that way. You came all this way and endured the impossible. You saved my life, and I refuse to let it be for nothing."

Tears welled in my eyes as I made a fist over my chest. I couldn't breathe.

"I wish to know you more. I wish to know our children and watch them grow," he said.

This was the man I'd come to love so deeply— soft underbelly, fiercely protective, and loyal. When he loved, he loved with everything he had. When he made a promise, he did everything in his power to keep it. It made me wonder how tormented he must've felt when he broke his vows to me in order to let Mack live. I couldn't help thinking that a part of him died that day, and he just couldn't bring it back, which was why he didn't remember me. *Self-preservation.*

"Mia! Oh fuck." Teddi rushed into the room, this time with Lema. "Oh fuck. Dammit, this is all your stupid stubborn fault! Why did you have to keep her from me?" she said to King.

"You said she was fine," he argued, his voice panicked. "Do something to help her."

"I said I *hoped* she'd be fine. And I can't fix this."

"Children." Lema stepped in. "Please cease your bickering and move out of my way." A moment later I felt her soothing warm hands on my chest, but it did little to help the pain or the lack of air in my lungs.

"She and the child are suffocating," Lema said.

"Fuck! Fuck! Fuck!" Teddi grabbed my hands and for a moment, I felt them heat up, but the warm light didn't reach into my chest. "Okay. Okay. I'm going to give you my ring." She began tugging it off her finger.

"No. Not safe," I groaned. The ring did not stop a person from dying, it simply rebooted their bodies after death, so they didn't stay dead. I had no clue what that would do to Ariadna. "I need a doctor."

"Mia, you must go back now," Lema said.

"She said she tried; it didn't work," Teddi pointed out.

"Try again, child," Lema demanded, placing a bundled Arch to my side. "Here, take her hand. You will leave with her." She put King's rough hand into mine, and he squeezed.

Our gazes met for a moment, and all I could see was warmth and affection in the blue depths of his eyes. He wanted to be with me.

My heart blew up like a big happy balloon. "Are you sure?" I whispered.

"I knew you were special the moment I saw you, Mia. I was simply too afraid to admit it."

Okay. We were doing this. I closed my eyes and tried to focus my mind away from the pain and on wanting to see us all safe and happy in my time, but nothing happened. I felt so tired, and Ariadna's little light felt colder.

"I can't," I whimpered in agony. "I'm too weak."

"Then we must ask the ancestors for help," said Lema, "but they will want a sacrifice, and—"

"Enough!" barked King. "All this talk is spending time she does not have."

I gasped for air, looking to Lema for help.

She closed her eyes.

After several moments, Teddi began prodding, "What are they saying?" But Lema remained in some meditative state.

"Hurry!" Teddi snapped.

Lema's dark eyes popped open. "They say…" She drew a deep breath. "It is as I told you. They say

Mia must make a sacrifice. She must give something up to gain something."

God, I just wanted to kick those dead Seers in their woman balls.

"Mia, you must choose something important to you." Even Lema looked worried now.

I suddenly felt like I was once again being played with, asked to make impossible choices between those I loved and held dear to my heart. Regardless, I would give my own life if it meant saving my unborn daughter, but that was not an option. She and I were not separable, and I sure as hell wasn't going to give up Arch. Not now. Not ever.

The pain unbearable, the tears flowed freely down the sides of my face. I looked at King, who stood tall behind Teddi and Lema. When our eyes met, he knew. He knew I had to give him up.

His lips parted with a sad little gasp or perhaps it was disappointment.

"I'm so sorry," I mouthed.

He moved Teddi out of the way. "No. I am sorry. I am sorry I wouldn't listen to you when you first arrived, but now you must listen to me. You will not make that trade with the Seers. You will focus. You will make yourself leave here this instant and go to this hospital place, and I will be there waiting for you on the other side."

I blinked at him, his words a mishmash I couldn't understand. "Where?" Did he mean death perhaps?

"You will leave right now, and I will be there."
He bent over me and squeezed my shoulder.

I didn't understand. "But that's not possible.
You can't—"

"Curses, woman! You can. If I've learned one
thing about you, it's that you have the obstinacy of
an ox. Now for once, do as you are told and leave."

"But how are you…" My mind clicked. *Shit.
Please, no more curses.* "No! You can't, King. Please,
I'm begging you."

"You must trust in me, Mia," he said.

My body screamed for more air and to help Ariadna. "No, please don't. You have no idea what
you're saying."

The only way for him to meet me on the other
side was to live, in one form or another, through the
next three thousand goddamned years.

He leaned down and whispered in my ear, "I
will make things different, and I will be there. I
promise. So please go and save our daughter."

As much as I wanted to plead with him, I didn't
have time. He would live in hell, feeling his soul rot,
consumed by rage and the darkness that comes
when you cannot escape your worst nightmare
because you are that nightmare. I would only get to
the other side and find the 10 Club still there, King
possibly still alive—evil as fuck and wanting to hurt
me, unable to protect our children because his heart
simply didn't feel love for anyone.

He pressed his forehead to mine. "I am sorry for doubting you, Mia. But now, you must have faith in me. We will get our time together, and I will ensure you are safe."

"You must let go of her now," Lema said. "Mia, try again. Focus."

With Arch tucked to my side, King bent down and kissed his tiny forehead. "See you soon, my little warrior."

King reluctantly stood up and backed away. Lema jerked her head at Teddi. "Put your hands over her stomach."

"What are we doing?" Teddi asked.

"You are going to give her your light." Lema jerked her head. "Hurry, child."

Teddi placed her trembling hands over Lema's. I looked into Teddi's eyes, wanting to say so many things—that I was so glad to have met her and would miss her if I survived. That she was like a sister and the time we had together, when I needed a friend the most, was something I'd never forget.

"Don't forget to write," I muttered.

Teddi laughed. "Tell my parents I love them."

I then looked at King's beautiful face. *Please don't do this.* But that was a lie. I would've given anything to see him again. I wasn't ready to let him go.

He flashed that charming, cocky smile as if to tell me one last time that it would all work out. Then I felt a warmth blanketing my body and my mind going dark. I thought of Ariadna safe and happy. I thought of Arch in his little crib. I imagined King and me walking on his favorite beach just outside our home, his warm living body close to mine beneath the sheets. *Go there. Go there. Your life depends on it.* I felt my body fading away, unsure if I was dying or returning home.

Then I was nothing.

CHAPTER TWENTY-ONE

I opened my eyes and found myself staggering on my parents' doorstep in San Francisco, Arch screaming bloody murder in my arms. At first I just wanted him to be quiet so my mind could rise above the pain or the fact I was spitting up blood. But it was his screaming that got my mother running to the front door.

"Jesus Christ," she yelled, scooping up Arch and leaning into me before I fell over. "Honey, call 9-1-1!" she yelled over her shoulder. "What happened, Mia. Can you speak?" She helped me land softly on the wooden porch.

"Punctured lung," I croaked.

"Oh, God. Oh, God. How did this happen?"

I didn't have an explanation, so I just said, "Is King here?"

"King? Who's King, sweetie?"

My heart crashed into a cold brick wall. I wanted to cry but could do little more than moan and writhe on the ground, trying to keep the oxygen flowing.

He's not here. He didn't make it. All the hope inside me drained away. For a moment, one stupid lousy moment, I had believed he would keep his word and we might start over.

"Why are you and Arch in those strange clothes?" my mother asked, her blue eyes filled with confusion. "I'm sorry. Don't talk. Don't talk." She shook her head.

My father came running out. "They're on their way." Luckily the hospital was little more than three blocks over.

Might not matter. I felt my vision blacking out, but I refused to let Hagne win this round. She might be the reason that King and I were once again robbed of another chance, but she would not be the reason this body stopped breathing or that I lost my sweet little Ariadna. I refused.

"Mom," I whispered, "tell them I'm pregnant." The paramedics needed to know in case I blacked out, which I didn't.

They arrived within minutes, and I stayed awake for the entire ride to the hospital. I stayed awake while they tried to clear my lungs and I felt my life slipping away.

But as they placed a mask over my mouth, I saw him—King's dark shadow looming behind the doctors and nurses frantically trying to keep me alive.

His ghost.

I smiled at him, thinking that in a way, maybe

he'd kept his promise. His spirit stuck around, waiting for me to die.

"Don't give up," I heard him whisper.

I blinked, and he was gone.

"Hurry! She's going," was the last thing I heard before the anesthesia took hold.

CHAPTER TWENTY-TWO

I woke up alone in a blurry fog, but the empty coffee cup on the bedside table told me my father or mother wasn't far.

My body in excruciating pain, I tried to take a full breath. I felt like I'd been beaten, put back together, and beaten up again. Then I noticed the tubes running from my nose and mouth. I immediately started to claw at my face, setting off a beeping sound, followed by a woman's voice telling me to stay still. It didn't take long for her to remove the crap in my throat.

"You had a lot of fluid in your lungs, but the bleeding has stopped," the nurse said.

"Arch," I whispered.

"I'm not sure, but your mother will be right back. She went for more coffee."

"My baby?"

The nurse pointed to the monitor, which I then realized was hooked up to my stomach. "Steady as a rock."

If it didn't hurt so much, I would've sighed with

relief.

My mind quickly went to the moments before my return home and of King pleading with me to have faith.

What went wrong? Why wasn't he here?

Maybe he'd come to his senses. After all, I'd begged him not to do it.

"Mia," my mother's voice rang through the room, instantly calming me, "oh, honey. It's so nice to see you awake. They said it would take days." She still wore her pajamas and had her blonde hair in a little ponytail. Her blue eyes, same color as mine, were bloodshot from crying.

"King. Are you sure he's not here?" I said in a raspy voice.

"Honey, I don't know anyone named King. What happened to you?"

"I don't remember," I lied.

"Well, the police were here and the doctors were asking all sorts of questions. They said you looked like you were cut from the inside out."

Teddi had only been able to heal the outside. I'm sure that confused the hell out of the doctors, but frankly who gave a shit? I was alive, and that meant Ariadna would be all right.

Just as I thought that, I felt a tiny flutter in my lower stomach.

There you are, sweetie. Mommy's so glad you're okay.

"Is Arch okay?" I asked with a labored breath.

"He's fussy after all of the tests the doctors did to make sure he wasn't injured, too. But everything's fine. He's with your father."

"Aren't you going to ask about me?" A deep, dark voice filled the room.

I looked behind my mother, and there, standing in an elegant black suit, was King.

My eyes teared up until my fear kicked in. I couldn't see his colors. I couldn't see if he was alive or good or bad.

I simply stared at him, waiting for him to say something.

"Would you mind giving me a moment alone with my wife?" he asked.

"I told you to call me Mom. But of course. I'll be right outside." My mother flashed a consoling smile and left.

King waited patiently for her to be out of earshot and then took a seat. "So, am I to assume that you know everything now?" There was a smugness to his smile.

I made a little nod.

"And you remember who I am, who I really am?" he asked.

I nodded again.

"I admit, after three thousand years, I expected a bit more excitement, Mia."

"But…but…" I didn't want to ask. My heart couldn't take any bad news.

Guessing my question, he whispered proudly,

"Yes. I am alive."

"But-but how?"

He lifted his hand and showed me his pinky ring. It had a diamond set into a solid gold band.

"Ohmygod," I whispered. "How did you get that?"

"Teddi gave it to me. And she sends her love. She also wrote you a ridiculous amount of letters, which I preserved for you. At least I hope so. It was not easy making wax-lined jars in 1400 BC."

That was when I noticed his blue, blue eyes. *Ohmygod. He is alive.* Tears of utter relief flooded my vision. Not only was he alive, but he did not seem like a complete wicked bastard.

He continued, "There is much to tell you, much that happened along the journey, but none of that is important right now. What matters is we are together, you are safe, and the children are safe."

"Are we really married?" I whispered. He'd said "wife" when he'd entered the room just now.

"The old Seer woman was right. The events aligned in such a way that enabled our paths to cross without any contradictions to the past." He leaned in and stroked my forehead. "We met a little over two years ago, and we've been married for almost as long. You had Arch about three months ago and got pregnant again almost right away. Guess my sperm is really strong." He leaned back and crossed his arms over his chest proudly.

"So I never knew who you really were?"

He slowly shook his head. "I have thoroughly enjoyed getting to know you, Mia, the one who lived before she went back in time to see me."

My head couldn't easily make sense of this all. If we'd really changed history, I suppose that meant the Mia he'd been with up until now had lived a completely different life. A happy life free from the past I'd endured. *So she kind of went away when I came back. This is such a trip.* I'd have to dive into that mind fuck of a mess later.

"Is 10 Club gone?" I asked.

"I promised you I would fix all this, didn't I?"

"Yes, but—"

"But nothing. You rest and heal, and I will tell you everything when you're ready." He took my hand and kissed it. "Simply know that you are safe now."

So we did it? We really did it? 10 Club was gone. King was a man and with me. My babies were okay. I just couldn't believe it. After so much hardship and pain, was it possible for my life to really end up in a perfect place?

Part of me didn't dare hope; I'd been let down so many times. The other part of me wanted to tap-dance. I deserved a happy ending. We deserved a happy ending. We'd fought like hell for it.

"Jesus, Mia! Mom says you were stabbed? What the hell?" From the doorway, a set of blue gray eyes gazed at me with irritation.

"Justin?" No. It couldn't be. "You're alive?"

Justin looked at King. "Did she hit her head?"

"It's the painkillers. She's a bit out of it," King replied.

Justin came around the other side of the bed, and all I could do was stare in wonder at my dead brother who was no longer dead. He was as beautiful as ever with his sandy blonde hair and dimples and boyish smile.

My heart leapt into my throat, triggering a little hiccup cry as I tried to breathe.

"Leave it to you, Mia, to make drama the day before I leave for Mexico," Justin said with a smirk. "Now I'll have to delay and—"

"Me-Mexico?"

He frowned. "I'm heading up my first dig. Remember? You really did take a beating. Was it a car that hit you?"

"So-something like that," I replied.

Justin's cell rang, and he grabbed it from his pocket. "One second. It's one of the guys on my crew." Justin stepped over by the doorway and began chatting about some lost equipment.

I looked at King, feeling terrified. "You can't let him go."

He smiled with the world's cockiest grin. "Mia, it's perfectly safe." He gave me a knowing look. "This I promise. Nothing that will lead to his death, and I am funding his expedition. I made sure everything would be as I promised."

I couldn't believe this.

He continued, "I had a very long time to think through my game plan. Now please get some rest. You and I have some getting to know each other, and I need to take you on our first date. Again." He chuckled. "This is going to take some getting used to."

"I don't ever think I will." Every wish I'd ever had was now a reality.

He reached out and ran his thumb along my bottom lip, beaming. "We have all the time in the world, my beautiful Mia."

CHAPTER TWENTY-THREE

Two weeks later, my body was on the road to recovery, though it would take time to be back to my old breathing self. Draco, as I would now have to get used to calling him, sat with me each day for a few hours, telling me everything that had happened over the last three thousand years. Holy hell, it was a lot. And he'd only given me the short version.

He said that after I left Minoa, things changed for him. He began to question his purpose, his role, and his entire life. It hadn't been easy for him to accept that he would have such a negative impact on the world when it contradicted who he believed he was—a king who deeply cared about his people.

"The truth was difficult to swallow," he'd said, "but once I accepted it, I realized I could choose who I wanted to become. You'd given me the gift of owning my fate."

So he set off to find himself, leaving Teddi and Mack and his people behind. He said he traveled to China and to South America and anywhere he could get to by boat, by horse, or on foot. "I stayed away from the Arctic, though. Too damned cold and thermal clothing did not exist, as you well know. But I went everywhere else."

I couldn't begin to imagine seeing the world at a time when people lived so isolated from each other. I imagined he'd run into a few unwelcoming, very scary people and his ring came in handy a few times.

"What happened to Teddi and Mack?"

King had shifted his tall frame in his seat when I'd asked that question. And despite looking uncomfortable as hell, he was still the most beautiful man I'd ever seen. This version of him, without the haunted past, had a levity and charm about him I never could've imagined. He was still King— arrogant, confident, and smart—but the menacing vibe was gone. Completely. I couldn't stop drinking him in every time he came by to sit with me in the hospital.

As for Mack and Teddi, King told the story like this: "When I finally returned to the island, they were old. They had six children, ten grandchildren, and two great-grandchildren."

"But you hadn't aged."

With nostalgia in his eyes, he shook his head. "I stayed with Mack until his last breath. He told me how grateful he was for having such a wonderful life. I truly believe he lived as he'd been destined to. A beloved king, husband, and father. When he died, he was surrounded by everyone he loved, including Teddi, who died shortly after."

The image of them dying brought tears to my eyes, but the thought of them living out their lives together made me happier than hell. "I wish I could've been there."

King cleared his throat. "Teddi made me promise to bring you the letters she wrote on handmade paper. She said it would make you feel like you hadn't missed out on anything."

That had made me smile. She'd wanted us to be close even though thousands of years separated us.

"Right after that, about the time their oldest son, Marias, took over as king, the Seers warned of a volcanic eruption, and everyone began planning to leave Crete and resettle elsewhere. I told them about the places I'd gone and seen, the people I'd met. The world was fairly uninhabited, so they had their pick of new homes."

"Where did they go?"

"They went to what is now known as Cyprus. It took them two years to move everyone, but they did it. A good thing. Less than a year later, there was an eruption on Santorini that would've killed everyone."

Amazing. If war hadn't wiped them out, the volcano would've. "You really did change history." I wondered what the impact was on the world now that Seers weren't extinct and 10 Club was gone. Evil people still existed and always would, of course, but at least the good guys would have a fighting chance. *A fair fight.*

King then explained that after Mack died and everyone he knew was gone, it had been a dark period of his life. He'd thought about taking off the ring and letting go, but the thought of seeing us again, of keeping his promise to me, gave him motivation to keep going. I wanted to ask if he'd found company—lovers, friends, other people—to pass the time with, but I realized he would tell me what he needed to share—what he thought was right. There were things I just didn't need to know.

"So how did you and I meet?" I asked.

"Teddi had told me the year you were born but did not know your exact birthday. She also knew you were from San Francisco. So I moved here around the turn of the century. I started a shipping business, importing spices, art, and furniture from around the world. And I waited. Then one day, I saw you crossing the street with your mother. You were just a little girl, but I recognized you right away."

"Ewww…you pervert."

He'd laughed at that. "It was a bit strange to see a five-year-old and say, 'Hey, there goes my wife.' However, I had waited this long, I could wait another twenty years. So I kept tabs on you but stayed away, not planning to attempt to meet you until your twenty-fifth birthday—which was your age when we met. But then one day, right before your birthday, you walked into my shop, looking for a gift for your brother. After that, I couldn't stay away. The way you looked at me—it was like you knew me, but you didn't."

"Now you know how I felt when I went to see you in Crete."

"Exactly. But I also knew that at some point, the past would catch up with us and that one day, you would become the woman I met three thousand years ago. Regardless, I fell in love with you. I knew I would still love you even after you changed."

"How's that working out for you?"

He shrugged. "You're okay."

I laughed. "Oh, I see how it is." But honestly, I knew this had to be strange for him. It was for me, too. We felt connected but didn't truly know each other. "So no 10 Club. No curses. No dead people being brought back to life to enslave the masses?"

"Afraid not. But I do have a business to run, and I've been neglecting things for weeks. Let's get you home and then I must leave for a few days. There's a collection of china and crystal in Italy I must inspect. The dealer will only hold it for me another few days before he sells the collection off to someone else."

"You're really an antiquities dealer?"

"I know a lot about old things." He smiled, and it lit up my heart. "So, are you ready to begin our new life?"

My words stuck in my throat. It seemed impossible to feel so happy. "You have no idea."

෴ ෴

After I checked out of the hospital, Draco took me by my parents' house to retrieve Arch, who looked plump, happy, and spoiled rotten. Goat milk and barley were not on the menu, so I'm sure that added to his sunny disposition.

Justin had already left for Mexico, but promised to be back in a few weeks for a visit. I couldn't wait to soak him up. It was a dream come true. All of it. My life complete.

We pulled up to the house, a renovated blue Victorian, and it was no surprise that it was on the same spot where King once had his creepy modern palace overlooking the Golden Gate Bridge. I had not told him this detail, but fate seemed to have repeated in some aspects. I didn't care. This house looked warm and cheerful with bright red roses in the front garden and colorful paint—purples and greens—around the base of the turrets and under the eaves.

King pulled the black Mercedes SUV—his car, also not a surprise—into the driveway, and I just sat there staring up at the fairytale house.

"Is something the matter?" King asked.

"No. Not at all. I'm trying to imagine us living here together." I looked into his blue, blue eyes.

He flashed his trademark smile. "For the record, you love it. Especially the master suite I had built for you on the top floor." He opened his door and walked around to help me out. "Shall we?"

I suddenly felt nervous. I knew this man, but it felt like our first date. "Ready."

He grabbed a snoozing Arch from the car seat, looking like an experienced father, totally comfortable handling him.

"You know, you look really hot with a baby in your arms."

He smiled. "You always say that."

"That's because you do." He looked hot without a baby in his arms, too.

We walked up to the front door, and King opened it up. "Just wait until I put on a blue skirt. That will blow your mind."

I laughed. "How is this possible?"

"What?" He held the door for me, and I entered, taking a whiff of the air. It smelled like home—Arch's baby powder, my perfume, even the vanilla air freshener candles I loved.

"You're so happy. I've never seen you like this."

He stepped in close, letting me catch the scent of his expensive cologne. Exactly the same he'd always worn. "I am not that other man, Mia. I keep my promises, and I always will."

He leaned down and kissed me. My body stilled as I took in the warmth of his lips. They felt silky and sensual as ever. It felt like kissing the man I'd fallen in love with so many years ago when he'd been just a man, deeply devoted and strong, but just a man.

My king. I pulled back and stared up at him.

"Is everything all right?" he asked, his voice velvety and deep.

"I think you need to go put that baby down and show me the master suite."

"Thought you'd never ask."

CHAPTER TWENTY-FOUR
KING

I could spend hours gazing into Mia's sky blue eyes, telling her how long I'd waited for this moment, of the hell I'd endured. But why waste my energy on talking when I could be with her, showing her how I felt?

I set our son into his crib and take Mia by the hand, guiding her up to the top floor, our private oasis filled with every luxury a woman could want—fireplace, sauna, walk-in closet. I spared no expense for her, knowing that this room would be where we would spend our time relearning each other. Fucking. Talking. Resting. And for me…pretending.

I help her up the last flight, knowing her body still needs to heal. But I need her more. I need the real her. The one with scars and grit. The one who knows pain and suffering as much as she knows love.

My Mia.

For her, I will keep my promise. She will live in

a safe world free from the insanity and violence of 10 Club.

I will never tell her the truth.

Because, you see, I did give up. I took off the ring. I ended my life thousands of years ago.

But something happened the moment I drew my final breath, the cold steel of the blade in my gut seared into my memories forever. I saw every second we'd lived now, then, and those moments that would never be when I had been cursed.

It is true what they say—your whole life flashes before your eyes when you die. But what no one tells you is that it truly is the whole. What could've been, what has been, what might be. I saw how I had tried a million different ways to be a good, good man and save the people I loved, only to end up destroying them and myself in the process. Mack, Mia, my people and children. Every move I made left everyone scathed.

There was only one move I hadn't tried.

And in that moment, able to see the pieces, I knew how much I loved Mia and that there wasn't anything in this world I wouldn't do for her.

Including the unthinkable.

I show Mia her new palace, only vaguely aware of what I'm saying about the work I've done on the house. In my mind, we're already in bed. I'm inside her, on top of her, kissing her sweet mouth and tasting her.

"This is just…" She draws a short breath, looking around the finely furnished room. "It's incredible."

"Enough sightseeing." Standing at the foot of the bed, I pull her body close and kiss her. Softly at first, so as not to scare her. She has no clue what I am, who I am.

Her soft body melts against me, and I wrap my arms around her, careful to hold her close but not hurt her. I've acquired many gifts over the centuries and my powerful body is one of them.

Our mouths mingle and our tongues dance, but that's not what I want. I quickly strip off her clothing—jeans and T-shirt—and watch while she removes her undergarments. Her creamy skin is paler than I remember, but I know in time she'll grow strong again.

"You're beautiful, Mia."

She blushes, standing before me nude.

"You're not so bad yourself." She flashes one of those coy, knowing smiles that feels like a familiar song—one I love.

"I can't believe you're finally here." I shed my pants and reveal my hard cock without hesitation.

She licks her lips and grins, just the way I knew she would.

"Shut up and fuck me," she says.

I don't need further encouragement, but I do know to be careful with her.

I quickly have her on the bed beneath me. I can't hear or see straight as I plunge my cock into her, feeling like it's the first time. Our bodies move and sweat and she groans softly in my ears as I push and withdraw my thick shaft.

A million thoughts run through me when she's pushing her hips into mine, trying to get my dick deeper. *You're mine. I will never share you or leave you. I will always protect you.*

The minutes fly by, and her body tenses. Her nails dig deep into my shoulders. The moment I hear her climaxing, the cum explodes from my cock. I think about how good she feels, how right she feels. I think about how I can't wait to make love to her again as soon as she's ready. Next time slower.

She sighs, and her arms fall limp to her sides. "That was incredible."

I smile to myself. This was all worth it. *As long as she never finds out the truth.*

I pull out and get up from the bed, knowing I've neglected a dozen phone calls in the last hour.

"Hey. Where do you think you're going?" Mia's heavy lids are almost closed.

"I'm going downstairs to get vitamin water," I say quietly, sliding on a pair of jeans, and glance at her stomach carrying our second child. "For the baby."

"Sounds good." Mia smiles, closes her eyes, and nestles into the bed.

"That's my girl. Be right back." I grab my cell, make my way down to the first floor into my study, and hit the send button. "It's me."

"For fuck's sake, King. You think I've got all fucking day waiting for you to answer your phone?"

Goddamned Seers. Always so mouthy. "Shut the hell up, Hagne."

"Or what?"

"Or I'll come and show you what happens to disobedient bitches who work for me."

She grumbles on the other end of the phone. I don't like being so crude with her, but whatever gets the job done.

"Fine. Sorry," she says. "So what's the next job?"

"I'll text you the address where he's hiding." The fucker has been on the run for weeks, but I am still the man who can find anything or anyone. For a price. And my price is Mia's happiness.

"He's dangerous, so be on your guard," I add.

"Always am."

Not really. However, that's the benefit of owning a chalice and having resurrected Seers at your beck and call. I can always bring them back if they are killed, and I can use the many gifts I've acquired to make them loyal. "Text me the moment he's dead."

"Fine." She hangs up, and I send her the location of a club member who's been sneaking around, trying to find out who runs 10 Club.

I do.

But now I run so much more than that.

You see, when I died, I understood how impossible it would be to have a world completely free of cruelty, evil, and darkness. There was a logic to 10 Club—creating an infrastructure to control and manipulate the bad things in this world, in lieu of allowing them to run rampant. But taming the monsters of this world would require a man with extraordinary power and gifts. Someone willing to accept the darkness in his soul.

Someone like me.

After all, how better to keep evil away from those I love than to understand it and become intimate friends with it? *Or, in my case, to rule it.*

So, it seems, I always was meant to be king. I simply had to accept my place in this world if I wanted to give Mia her happy ending. But there's nothing a man won't do for the woman he's destined to love. Including being a little bit evil.

THE END

AUTHOR'S EVIL NOTE

Hi, All!

I hope you enjoyed the twisty road and dark surprises! It's funny how when I envisioned this story about 10 Club, I always saw it leading back to the very beginning in order for King and Mia to truly be free and happy. In my mind, it had to be a sort of do-over where they got to rebuild their love from scratch and do it their way.

What I didn't see happening in this story, and neither did you, was a lot of sex. Now, I know some people feel like ya just can't have a romance novel without a ton o' steamy scenes. Others don't like the sex scenes at all; they just want a good story.

For me, however, I always feel like it can be raunchy and steamy or sweet and "fade to black" as long as it goes with the story. (Example: *Pride and Prejudice* v. *Fifty Shades*. Love them both.) That's why from me you'll see lots of steam in one book and not much in another. I treat each story like a unique creation that's just got to be told how it's got to be told, regardless of formulas or rules.

So I hoped you enjoyed! Personally, I hate to see the series end, but I love seeing everyone get their happy ending (I mean that both ways). Plus, I love that King stayed just a little bit evil. After all, that's why we love him. (Bad boys are the best!)

Anyway, I've got some sexy EVIL KING bookmarks for you (while supplies last). As always, DO mention if you took the time to write a review! I'll include an extra thank-you goody.

EMAIL: mimi@mimijean.net

And for all you Romantic Comedy fans, keep an eye out for the next Happy Pants Series book, LEATHER PANTS!! Yes, it's coming out MARCH 3 (2017) now. Yippy!
www.mimijean.net/leather-pants.html

Until then, happy reading, everyone!

Mimi

What songs kept my writer-tank fueled for this book? Here's my EVIL PLAYLIST!

"Jar Of Hearts" by Christina Perri
"F*ck You" by Lily Allen
"Save Me" by Jem
"Your Woman" by White Town
"Somebody That I Used To Know" by Gotye
"I Always Knew" by Jem
"The Way I Am" by Ingrid Michaelson
"Stopwatch Hearts" (feat. Emily Haines) by Delerium
"Dirty Laundry" by Bitter:Sweet
"The Fear" by Lily Allen
"Everything's Okay" by Lenka
"Heathens" by twenty one pilots
"Pumpkin Soup" by Kate Nash
"Mercy" by Duffy
"I'm Gonna Be (500 Miles)" by The Proclaimers
"The World At Large" by Modest Mouse
"Possibility" by Lykke Li
"All These Things That I've Done" by The Killers
"Cecilia And The Satellite" by Andrew McMahon in
    the Wilderness
"Lottery" by Train
"Play That Song" by Train
"My Type" by Saint Motel
"Cold Cold Man" by Saint Motel

COMING March 3, 2017

Book #3, The Happy Pants Café Series

It Only Takes One Hot Rock Star To Ruin Your Life…

The youngest woman to ever sit on the bench, the Honorable Sarah Rae Alma has busted her butt to get where she is. No fun. No distractions. And definitely no bad boys. In fact, she takes a certain pleasure in crushing their souls—yes, she has her reasons.

So when rock-n-roll's most famous bad boy, the legendary Colton Young, enters her court, looking hotter than sin and smugger than hell, she's just itching to serve a little justice.

But Sarah's about to make the biggest mistake of her life. And her fate will land squarely in the hands of the world's most notorious rock star rebel.

Will he crush her? Or will he tempt her to take a walk on the wild side?

FOR EXCERPTS, BUY LINKS, AND MORE:

www.mimijean.net/leather-pants.html

EVIL ACKNOWLEDGEMENTS

BIG EVIL HUGS!!! to the souls who put on their dark and wicked hats every time I write one of these non-snarky King books. Thank you Karen, Dali, Ally, and Naughty Nana for helping me get the plot rolling smoothly. Thank you, Latoya, Pauline, and Paul for taking time out of your lives to make my books sparkle (and get out on time). I am evilly grateful.

As always, a big thanks to my guys—angels every one of you! I know it suck sometimes to have a wife and mom who's a crazy writer. Never a day off.

Evil Kingly Wishes,
Mimi

ABOUT THE EVIL AUTHOR

MIMI JEAN PAMFILOFF is a *USA Today* and *New York Times* bestselling romance author. Although she obtained her MBA and worked for more than fifteen years in the corporate world, she believes that it's never too late to come out of the romance closet and follow your dream. Mimi lives with her Latin lover hubby, two pirates-in-training (their boys), and the rat terrier duo, Snowflake and Mini Me, in Arizona. She hopes to make you laugh when you need it most and continues to pray daily that leather pants will make a big comeback for men.

Sign up for Mimi's mailing list for giveaways and new release news!

STALK MIMI:
www.mimijean.net
twitter.com/MimiJeanRomance
pinterest.com/mimijeanromance
instagram.com/mimijeanpamfiloff
facebook.com/MimiJeanPamfiloff

Made in the USA
Middletown, DE
05 March 2017